Curious as to why everyone's attention had been caught so completely, Kit glanced over her shoulder, checking out the newcomer as he closed the door.

It only took her a moment to recognize the tall, dark, handsome man, his curly black hair a shade too long, his bright blue eyes vivid in his tanned face.

So, too, it seemed, did all local residents in the diner. Hearty greetings echoed around the room as one of Belle's most favored sons moved slowly down the diner's center aisle, a charmingly boyish grin on his smoothly shaven face.

Standing all but frozen to the spot, her hands clenched at her sides, Kit eyed him with a growing sense of dread. In that instant she wanted more than anything to take Nathan from his playpen and hurry out the back door of the diner just as quickly as she could.

Her more sensible self knew that taking such action would be foolhardy, though.

She could run from Simon Gilmore now, but she wouldn't be able to hide from him forever.

Dear Reader,

It's that time of year again—back to school! And even if
you've left your classroom days far behind you, if you're
like me, September brings with it the quest for everything
new, especially books! We at Silhouette Special Edition are
happy to fulfill that jones, beginning with *Home on the Ranch*
by Allison Leigh, another in her bestselling MEN OF THE
DOUBLE-C series. Though the Buchanans and the Days had
been at odds for years, a single Buchanan rancher—Cage—
would do anything to help his daughter learn to walk again,
including hiring the only reliable physical therapist around.
Even if her last name did happen to be Day....

Next, THE PARKS EMPIRE continues with Judy Duarte's
The Rich Man's Son, in which a wealthy Parks scion, suffering
from amnesia, winds up living the country life with a single
mother and her baby boy. And a man passing through
town notices more than the *passing* resemblance between
himself and newly adopted infant of the local diner waitress,
in *The Baby They Both Loved* by Nikki Benjamin. In
A Father's Sacrifice by Karen Sandler, a man determined
to do the right thing insists that the mother of his child marry
him, and finds love in the bargain. And a woman's search for
the truth about her late father leads her into the arms of a
handsome cowboy determined to give her the life her dad
had always wanted for her, in *A Texas Tale* by Judith Lyons.
Last, a man with a new face revisits the ranch—and the
woman—that used to be his. Only, the woman he'd always
loved was no longer alone. Now she was accompanied by a
five-year-old girl...with very familiar blue eyes....

Enjoy, and come back next month for six complex and
satisfying romances, all from Silhouette Special Edition!

Gail Chasan
Senior Editor

Please address questions and book requests to:
Silhouette Reader Service
U.S.: 3010 Walden Ave., P.O. Box 1325, Buffalo, NY 14269
Canadian: P.O. Box 609, Fort Erie, Ont. L2A 5X3

The Baby They Both Loved

NIKKI BENJAMIN

SPECIAL EDITION®

Published by Silhouette Books

America's Publisher of Contemporary Romance

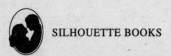

SILHOUETTE BOOKS

ISBN 0-373-24635-8

THE BABY THEY BOTH LOVED

Visit Silhouette Books at www.eHarlequin.com

Printed in U.S.A.

NIKKI BENJAMIN

was born and raised in the Midwest, but after years in the Houston area, she considers herself a true Texan. Nikki says she's always been an avid reader. (Her earliest literary heroines were Nancy Drew, Trixie Belden and Beany Malone.) Her writing experience was limited, however, until a friend started penning a novel and encouraged Nikki to do the same. One scene led to another, and soon she was hooked.

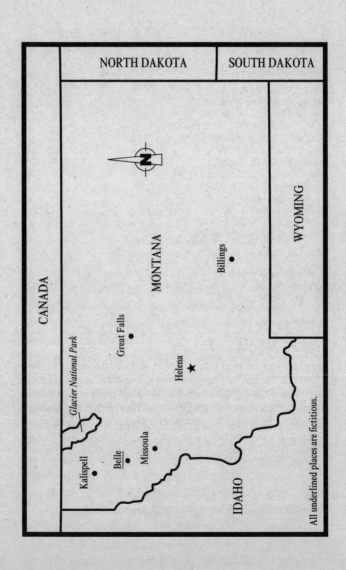

CANADA

NORTH DAKOTA

SOUTH DAKOTA

WYOMING

MONTANA

Billings

Glacier National Park

Great Falls

Helena ★

Kalispell

Belle

Missoula

IDAHO

All underlined places are fictitious.

Chapter One

Kit Davenport eyed the clock on the kitchen wall of the Dinner Belle Diner as she dumped handfuls of freshly chopped vegetables into the pot of stew meat already simmering on the six-burner stove. It was almost ten-thirty, and her part-time waitress, Bonnie Lennox, wasn't scheduled to start work until eleven.

Normally Bonnie came in when the diner opened its doors for breakfast at seven in the morning, but that day her young daughter was graduating from kindergarten, an event Kit hadn't wanted her to miss. Unfortunately, the diner's crusty old cook, George Ortiz, had called to say he, too, would be late that day due to a painful flare-up of the arthritis that occasionally crippled his gnarled hands and creaky knees but never his indomitable spirit.

Handling the Dinner Belle single-handedly wasn't a new experience for Kit. Since her mother, Dolores, had owned and operated the little diner in the small town of

Belle, Montana, until her death this past December, Kit had literally grown up there. So early in the tourist season, with nearby Glacier National Park's Logan's Pass not yet open to vehicular traffic, the breakfast crowd, made up mostly of locals she knew on a first-name basis, had also been relatively undemanding.

Kit had been able to take orders, fry eggs, flip pancakes, bus tables and wash dishes without a problem. But getting a head start on the lunch specials she and George had agreed upon for that Tuesday afternoon had been a bit of a challenge. Following even the simplest of her mother's recipes involved a lot more time and mental energy than she had to spare, especially when she also had to keep an eye on her two-year-old godson, Nathan Kane.

Though easily entertained by the constant activity going on all around him, as the morning wore on the little boy had been growing more and more unhappy with his confinement in the playpen she had set up for him in a corner by the counter.

Taking a peek at the pans of lasagna, a Dinner Belle favorite, baking in the double oven, Kit made a mental note to start defrosting the loaves of garlic bread still in the freezer. But first she had another breakfast plate to serve up. She slid the eggs out of the cast-iron skillet, added several rashers of bacon, a scoop of hash-brown potatoes and two freshly baked biscuits, then made a beeline for the kitchen doorway.

"Just a little longer, sweet boy," she cooed to Nathan, shooting a smile his way as she hurried past the playpen.

He called after her in his own special brand of gibberish, his high, young voice more aggrieved than it had been the last time she'd walked through the kitchen doorway.

He also waved his favorite stuffed teddy bear at her in an attempt to draw her attention to him rather than her customers. She didn't dare stop to acknowledge the gesture, though. That would only cause his fussiness to escalate another notch.

"He's such a good child," Winifred Averill commented as Kit set the plate on the elderly woman's table. "Shame about his momma, but that Lucy Kane always was a wild thing. Lucky for her she had you for a friend. Otherwise there's no telling what might have happened to that little boy."

"Yes, ma'am, Nathan is a good child," Kit agreed, trying not to bristle at Winifred's judgmental tone. She was well into her eighties, had lived her entire life in the small town of Belle and hadn't ever had a shy bone in her body. Her tendency toward plainspokenness could often be unsettling, but she had never been intentionally malicious. "And I was the lucky one to have had Lucy for my friend. She brightened my life with her fun-loving ways, and she truly cared about Nathan. I was honored when she asked me to be his godmother and named me as his guardian in her will."

"Hard to believe how his daddy's shirked all responsibility, and him coming from such a fine family, not to mention seeming like such a fine young man himself."

"Yes, it is hard to believe," Kit replied.

"Too bad he can't grow up here in Belle. But you were never as happy in this little town as your momma, or his momma, for that matter. Always had a yen for the big city, didn't you, Miss Kit?"

"Yes, ma'am."

"You were dead set on going away to college and you found a way to do it. Won a scholarship, got your undergraduate degree, then started working on a master's degree, your momma said. Majoring in psychology so you could listen to folks talk about their problems. Just like your momma did here at the Dinner Belle, and she didn't need any fancy college degree to give good advice. " Chuckling softly, Winifred Averill stirred her eggs into her potatoes, adding, "I sure am going to miss this place when you close up at the end of the summer."

"I'm hoping to have a buyer before then so closing up won't be necessary. In fact, I've already had a few inquiries," Kit said.

Two, to be exact, and neither couple had pursued their interest in the diner beyond an initial inquiry. But she wasn't about to set Mrs. Averill off again by admitting as much aloud.

Kit didn't want to have to close the Dinner Belle for good. But neither did she want to give up the life she'd made for herself in Seattle to run a diner in a small Montana town for the rest of her God-given days. She had gladly taken a leave from her graduate studies at the University of Washington to help out at home when her mother first became ill, and she had stayed on after her mother's death for the sole purpose of keeping the diner going until it could be sold. Then Lucy had been killed in a tragic accident on an icy back road, and suddenly Kit had also had a precious little boy to raise all on her own.

"Couple of years ago I would have bought the place myself," Winifred continued, interrupting Kit's reverie. "But I don't have as much energy now as I did when I was eighty-five."

"That's understandable, ma'am." Kit hid a smile as she met the woman's gaze. "Would you like more coffee?"

"Just a smidgen to warm up my cup, if it isn't too much trouble."

"No trouble at all."

As Kit turned to get the coffeepot from the warmer behind the counter, the tinkle of the little bell on the diner's front door announced the arrival of another customer. Likely just another local, she thought, eager to refill Mrs. Averill's coffee cup and get back to the kitchen.

She hadn't gone very far when the murmur of voices among the other customers sitting in the diner stilled, and into the silence Winifred Averill's voice rang out, loud and clear.

"Well, well, well…speak of the devil," she said, sounding not only amazed, but also quite pleased.

Curious as to why everyone's attention had been caught so completely, not to mention what had prompted Winifred's comment, Kit glanced over her shoulder, checking out the newcomer as he closed the door, then paused a long moment to survey the friendly faces turned his way.

It took Kit only a moment to recognize the tall, dark, handsome man, his curly black hair a shade too long, his bright blue eyes vivid in his tanned face, not a spare ounce of fat on his rangy body. So, too, it seemed, did all the local residents in the diner. Hearty greetings echoed around the room, accompanied by handshakes here and there, as one of Belle's most favored sons moved slowly down the diner's center aisle, a charmingly boyish grin on his smoothly shaven face.

Simon Gilmore took his own sweet time responding to one and all in a low voice laced with good humor. Standing near Winifred Averill's table, all but frozen to the spot, her hands clenched at her sides, Kit eyed him with a growing sense of dread. In that instant she wanted more than anything to take Nathan from his playpen and hurry out the back door of the diner just as quickly as she could.

Her more sensible self knew that taking such action would be foolhardy, though. She could run from Simon Gilmore now, but she wouldn't be able to hide from him forever. Behaving in a cowardly manner would only give him a weapon he could use against her. And, she reminded herself as she took a steadying breath, he could very well have any number of reasons for returning to Belle that didn't involve Nathan Kane.

Three years ago, Simon hadn't been able to get out of town fast enough when he'd found out Lucy was pregnant. And he hadn't been back since. More importantly, neither he nor his wealthy parents had ever acknowledged their relationship to the little boy. They hadn't contributed to his support while Lucy was alive. And in the three months since her death, neither Mitchell and Deanna, owners of one of the largest and most prosperous cattle ranches in the state, nor their only child, Simon, had come forward to claim the little boy.

There was Lucy's last will and testament to consider, as well. She had wanted Kit to be the one to raise her child should she be unable to do so herself, and in a surprising act for one normally so happy-go-lucky, she had stated as much in her will.

Although Kit's formal adoption of Nathan had yet to be finalized by the court, as far as she was concerned, he was already her child in every way that counted. Anyone who tried to take him away from her—including Simon Gilmore—would be in for a fight.

No amount of determination could completely overcome the shock of seeing Simon again, however. The steely core of resolution that had developed deep within her over the years wouldn't allow Kit to be intimidated by him. But at the same time she couldn't deny a lingering sense of vulnerability toward him—a vulnerability firmly rooted in the past.

Lucy hadn't been the only one attracted to Simon Gilmore all those years ago. But the memory of how Simon had toyed with her best friend's affection on and off for several years, only to dump her unceremoniously when he found out she was carrying his child, was all Kit needed to gather her scattered wits about her. With a grim twist of her lips, she straightened her spine, unwilling to be intimidated by someone so callow and insensitive.

Almost upon her, Simon finally met her gaze for the first time since he'd entered the diner. He stopped dead and did a double take that Kit would have actually found amusing under other circumstances. Then he moved toward her with a determined glint in his eyes, his grin suddenly wolfish.

Her stomach fluttering unnaturally, Kit stared at him, her mind suddenly muddled, unable to move or to speak.

Halting again only inches from her, Simon put his hands on her shoulders and drew her even closer.

"Well, hey, Miss Kit Davenport…what a surprise to see you here, and a damned nice one, too," he said, his deep voice shooting up an octave in seemingly honest amazement. "I do believe I've missed your pretty face, little darling."

Then, to Kit's utter dismay, Simon Gilmore bent his head and kissed her smack on the mouth as if they were long lost lovers blissfully meeting again. And so shocked was she that for just the merest instant her eyes closed instinctively and she almost, *almost,* kissed him back.

Only Winifred Averill's delighted cackle saved Kit from demeaning herself that completely. Going rigid, she jerked her head back at the same time she put her hands on Simon's chest and shoved him forcefully away.

"Don't," she said, her voice low, making no attempt at all to hide her anger. "Just don't do that, okay?"

"Hey, I'm sorry," he hastened to say, the look on his face now one of confusion as he tucked his hands in the back pockets of his jeans. "I didn't mean any harm. It's just so good to see you again, Kit. I guess I got a little carried away."

"No harm done," she replied in a calmer, slightly conciliatory tone as she took another step away from him. Not quite able to meet his gaze, she added, "You just caught me off guard."

She didn't want to cause any more of a scene in front of Winifred Averill and the other locals than she already had. Nor did she want to behave toward Simon in an overtly hostile manner. She couldn't afford to make an enemy of him until she knew exactly why he'd returned to Belle.

"I apologize," he said meekly enough, though his smile was wholly unrepentant. "It's just so good to see you again. Are you helping out at the diner for the summer, or just making a quick visit home?"

Doing her best to ignore the obvious appreciation in his bright blue eyes as he looked her up and down, not to mention her own womanly response to him, Kit considered instead the question he'd asked. Hadn't Simon heard about her mother's death? And if he didn't know about Dolores's death, was it possible he didn't know about Lucy's death, either?

It was, Kit realized. His parents traveled a lot, especially during the winter months. In fact, she couldn't remember seeing them around town much after the holidays. Although she had run into Mitchell Gilmore at the hardware store about a week ago, and she'd had Nathan with her then.

Never one to believe in coincidence, Kit had to fight the urge to look over at the playpen sitting in a corner near the counter. Instead she directed her gaze Simon's way, trying not to seem either completely welcoming or unwelcoming toward him.

"I'm here for the summer," she said, then gestured to an empty table, hoping to ward off any more questions. He could catch up on the latest news when he got to the Double Bar S. "Why don't you have a seat and take a look at the menu while I bring you some coffee?"

"I'd rather sit at the counter if you don't mind."

"Suit yourself."

Kit shrugged and turned away, but not before she saw Simon's smile fade, and a puzzled look replace the admiration that had brightened his brilliant blue eyes.

As he slouched onto one of the stools, Kit moved behind the counter. She still didn't dare to risk a glance in Nathan's direction for fear she would direct Simon's interest that way, as well. She couldn't hide the little boy from him forever, but there was no sense doing anything to stir the pot any sooner than absolutely necessary.

"What can I get for you?" she asked, adopting a matter-of-fact tone.

"Coffee, please," he requested, then added with the barest hint of sarcasm, "but only if it isn't too much trouble."

"No trouble at all," Kit replied.

Taking the coffeepot from the warmer, Kit remembered guiltily that she'd said the same thing to Winifred Averill and had yet to refill the elderly woman's cup. But then, Mrs. Averill had probably been so entertained by Kit's exchange with Simon that she hadn't even noticed.

"Do you want to order breakfast, too?"

Trying to sound a little friendlier, she set a sturdy white china mug on the counter. She wanted Simon out of the diner as soon as possible, but she was afraid that she'd rouse his suspicion if she acted too much out of character.

"No, thanks. Just coffee will do. I'm expected at the ranch before noon, but I couldn't drive through town without stopping here first." He paused a moment and looked around the diner, a thoughtful expression on his face. "This place sure does bring back a lot of good memories."

"I'm sure it does," Kit agreed, unable to avoid injecting a note of sarcasm into *her* tone.

Turning away, she grabbed the handle of a freshly brewed pot of coffee and a couple of packets of creamer. She tossed the packets on the counter and tipped the pot to fill Simon's mug.

At the same instant, Nathan let out a mighty squall of discontent, signaling that he'd had just about as much time in the playpen as he could handle. Startled, Kit splashed hot coffee on the counter, barely missing Simon's hand. A moment of silence settled over the diner, followed by a ripple of laughter among the customers still left there, most of whom were used to Nathan's occasional and understandable demands for attention.

"Sorry," Kit murmured, taking a damp cloth from under the counter.

As she mopped up the mess she'd made, she watched

Simon surreptitiously from under her lowered lashes. He had been as startled as she by the child's cry, and quite naturally he had looked over at the playpen, seeming to notice it for the first time since he'd sat at the counter.

Initially, the expression on his face was one of curiosity. But then his features shifted, reflecting surprise, and then genuine confusion.

It was one thing to see a little boy standing in a playpen, in a place where you'd never seen one in the past, waving a teddy bear at you. It was something else altogether to see a little boy with silky black curls and brilliant blue eyes—a little boy who was, obviously and undeniably, a much smaller, much younger image of your very own self.

Kit clutched the coffee-soaked cloth in both hands, now staring openly at Simon as the color drained from his face. He made a sound, low in his throat and unintelligible to her ears. Finally he shifted his gaze to her once again. Still seemingly bewildered, he stared at her wordlessly for several interminable seconds.

To Kit, the resemblance between father and son was impossible to miss. Yet Simon didn't seem to get the connection. Or maybe he just didn't want to get it, she thought with a hot flash of anger.

"So, Kit, you've had a new addition to your family?" he asked at last, an odd croak in his voice as he gestured in Nathan's general direction.

"In a way, yes," Kit replied, barely managing to hide her annoyance.

He had to be in deep denial to think Nathan was her biological child. That kiss on the lips he'd given her a few minutes ago was the closest *she* had ever gotten to having sex with him. How could he possibly think she'd produced a child who looked just like him?

"The little boy in the playpen is your son, then," he said, visibly relaxing as he sat back on his stool.

"He is now."

"What do you mean by that? Is he your son or isn't he?" Again, Simon seemed confused and just a little exasperated.

Her anger flaring once more, Kit directed a hard look Simon's way. He just didn't get it—more likely didn't *want* to get it. But eventually he would, now that he was back in town.

Though Lucy had never broadcast the identity of Nathan's father, once Nathan had begun to develop distinctive features it was clear that the baby could, in fact, be Simon's. It wouldn't take long for someone to yank Simon out of his blissful, self-indulgent ignorance. Disgusted as she was with him, Kit didn't see any reason why she shouldn't be that someone.

"Nathan is my son now," she said again. "But Lucy Kane was his birth mother. Unfortunately, she was killed in an automobile accident at the end of February. I'm his legal guardian and I've been taking care of him ever since." She took a deep breath, trying to shake the nervous quiver from her voice. "I've also taken the necessary steps to adopt him, and according to my attorney, Isaac Woodrow, the court will likely approve my petition within the next few weeks."

"That little boy is Lucy Kane's son?" Simon repeated slowly.

His astonishment was more than evident as his gaze shifted from Kit to Nathan, then back to Kit again. She doubted he had heard what she'd said about the adoption.

"Yes, he's Lucy's son."

"But Lucy was killed in an automobile accident in February?"

Simon repeated her words yet again, appearing to be even more stunned.

"She was out late at night, heading home from a party at a house on Flat Head Lake. Her car hit a patch of black ice. She skidded off the road and hit a tree.

Simon looked as if he'd been dealt a physical blow. His face paled even more as he gripped the counter with both hands. Undeniable anguish shadowed his vivid blue eyes. He seemed to be not only stunned, but also badly shaken as his gaze shifted to Nathan yet again.

He tried to speak and failed. Then, without another word to Kit, he pushed away from the counter, turned on his heel and strode to the front door of the diner. He paused there, head bent and shoulders slumped, his hand on the knob. Finally, he glanced back at Nathan one last time. Then he opened the door and walked out.

Kit wasn't sure how she had expected Simon to respond to her revelations. Listening to the echo of the door slamming shut, she knew only that the pain shadowing his gaze in those last moments before he'd left hadn't been feigned. In fact, the honesty of his anguish had taken her totally and completely by surprise.

She had already acknowledged the possibility that he hadn't heard about Lucy's death. And considering his past history with her, Kit had assumed the news would cause him at least a small measure of dismay. But the look on his face had revealed a much deeper torment.

How could that possibly be when he had abandoned Lucy almost three years ago, then hadn't shown the least bit of interest in her welfare or that of his child any time since?

In fact, Simon's reaction had been more in line with that of a man who had not only just discovered that he had a son, but also that the love of his life had died. That level of devastation didn't make the least bit of sense to Kit. She knew that Lucy had told Simon she was pregnant. Lucy had said as much to Kit three years ago. And instead of providing for Lucy and the baby, Simon had left her to cope alone.

How could he now act like the injured party? It just didn't make any sense.

And, of course, he *would* walk away without a single word of explanation. Although that particular response wasn't quite as surprising to Kit as it could have been. He *had* walked away from his responsibilities once already, and he had stayed away three long years.

Only this time Kit had a feeling Simon Gilmore wasn't going to disappear completely. There had been something about the look in his eyes before he'd finally left the diner that had warned her he would be back again. He would want to think before he acted, but when he acted—

"So the prodigal son has come back to town, and about time, too," Winifred Averill said as she stepped up to the counter. "Can't say I'm surprised. 'Course, he didn't stick around here very long once he caught sight of the youngster, did he?"

"Not very long at all," Kit agreed.

Drawn from her reverie, she tossed the damp cloth into the sink under the counter and crossed to the cash register to ring up the elderly woman's bill.

"Sorry I never got back to your table with the coffeepot."

"I didn't really need any more caffeine. I'm jittery enough as it is. Anyway, you had your hands full." Mrs. Averill chuckled as she dug her coin purse from the pocket of her denim jacket.

"Yes, actually I did."

"I expect he'll be back soon enough. Best you be prepared," the elderly woman advised with a knowing look, as she paid her bill.

The ding of the bell over the diner's front door as Winifred turned away from the counter had Kit looking up with apprehension. She knew she would have to face Simon again eventually, but she had hoped it wouldn't be quite so soon.

To her relief, it was Bonnie Lennox, her friend and part-time waitress, who sailed into the diner, her blond curls bouncing on her shoulders, her brown eyes bright and cheerful.

"Hello, all," Bonnie called out.

The few remaining customers sent out a chorus of greetings, while Mrs. Averill gave her a friendly pat on the arm as she passed by on her way out. Kit shot her friend a grateful smile, then crossed to the playpen, scooped Nathan into her arms and gave him a hug.

"Busy morning?" Bonnie asked as she grabbed a red apron from the hook just inside the kitchen doorway and tied it over her denim skirt and navy T-shirt.

"Not too bad. How was Allison's graduation?"

"She looked so cute in her little cap and gown, and she won an award for best artwork." Bonnie's grin couldn't have been any prouder, but then a worried frown creased her forehead as her expression turned serious. "I thought I saw Simon Gilmore sitting in a black SUV parked at the curb half a block down the street. Were my eyes deceiving me, or has he dared to show his handsome face in town again?"

"Oh, he's definitely back in town. In fact, he was just in the Dinner Belle a few minutes ago," Kit said.

"And?" Bonnie prompted, eyeing Kit with obvious dismay.

"He didn't know about Lucy."

"Did he see Nathan?"

"Yes, he saw Nathan, but he seemed really…shocked. Like he didn't know his own son existed."

"How could that possibly be?"

"I don't honestly know. But the way he acted today didn't jibe at all with the way Lucy said he acted three years ago."

"What did he say?" Bonnie asked.

"Not a lot," Kit replied. "Mostly he just asked questions. He seemed surprised by my answers, too. Very surprised. But he didn't offer an explanation of any kind. He just got up and left without a word."

"Do you think he'll cause a problem with Nathan's adoption?"

"I don't know," Kit answered, averting her gaze as she headed back to the kitchen, Bonnie trailing after her in sympathetic silence.

Only she had a feeling—a bad feeling—that she *did* know, and what she knew had her holding on to Nathan just a little tighter and with a lot more anxiety than she ever had before.

Chapter Two

Several realizations spun out one after another in Simon Gilmore's mind, rolling and tumbling into a stunning confusion of incredibly unbelievable information. Time ticked away slowly, one minute to the next, but he couldn't stir himself to do anything more than sit at the steering wheel of his shiny new SUV and stare out the windshield, his gaze unfocused.

With a few devastatingly simple statements, Kit Davenport had turned his blissful little world upside down. Seeing her in the diner had triggered a youthful exuberance in him, and kissing her had seemed only natural. But then she'd brought him up to date quickly and concisely. Each of her revelations had been upsetting individually—taken altogether, the intensity of them had numbed him, heart and soul.

To hear that lovely, lively Lucy Kane had died suddenly, tragically, in an automobile accident saddened

Simon deeply. Though she cut him to the quick three years ago, they had shared a lot of good times together. And lately the pain of their last parting had tempered so that the mere thought of her no longer caused his gut to twist in anguish.

He had actually been looking forward to seeing her again during his unexpected and hastily arranged trip home. Finally ready to move past her betrayal of his trust, he had hoped to gain the closure he needed to the relationship they'd once shared.

But he was never going to see Lucy Kane again, and there would be no closure for him now. Instead he found himself standing on the edge of a precipice with unforeseen and truly incredible possibilities opening out before him.

Simon had seen enough photographs of himself at an early age to know that the little boy he'd seen in the Dinner Belle Diner was his spitting image. He was also living proof that Lucy's betrayal had been so much more deliberate and so much more despicable than he'd ever imagined.

Nathan Kane had to be the child Lucy had carried during her pregnancy three years ago. But Lucy had looked him in the eye that long-ago August night and insisted the baby wasn't his. She had urged him—oh-so-blithely—to accept the job he'd been offered as a photojournalist for the *Seattle Post* following his graduation from graduate school. She had even said that he shouldn't give her or the baby another thought because there was someone else in her life she had come to love more than him.

Had Lucy been telling him the truth as she thought she knew it? Simon wondered now. Had she really been having sex with another man that summer? She'd been so sure he wasn't the one to get her pregnant, and he had been careful about using condoms…most of the time. Or had she lied to him intentionally?

Simon had wanted to marry Lucy three years ago and take her with him to Seattle, and Lucy had seemed to want what he wanted during those long, lazy days of their last summer together. But then she had dropped her bombshell on him. Not only was she pregnant, she was pregnant with another man's child.

Devastated, Simon had gone away to lick his wounds, and he had stayed away till now, feigning disinterest in his hometown and the people there whenever one or the other of his parents brought up the subject.

His parents—

Muttering a curse under his breath, Simon understood at last the urgency behind his father's insistence that he return to Belle immediately to take care of "family business." Mitchell Gilmore hadn't bothered to explain in detail the exact nature of the business. He had simply ordered Simon to come home at once, an order his mother, Deanna, had issued, as well, her tone holding an angry edge he'd never heard in her voice even during the most rambunctious of his teenage years.

Luckily he'd had vacation time coming—almost four weeks accumulated over the past couple of years. Traveling all over the world to shoot photographs and to write stories for the paper, he hadn't really wanted or needed to get away from the office the way many of his fellow journalists did.

A good thing, too, he admitted now. Sorting out the situation he faced here in Belle was definitely going to take more than the week he'd originally anticipated having to spend at the ranch.

Simon had known a confrontation of some sort would be awaiting him when he arrived at the spacious, sprawling, one-story house built of cedar logs and stone twenty miles east of town. That was the main reason why he'd stopped first at the Dinner Belle Diner for a last bracing cup of coffee, a plate of eggs and bacon and a couple of Dolores Davenport's homemade buttermilk biscuits.

No matter what news his parents had for him, he would have been better able to deal with it after a late breakfast at the diner where he'd enjoyed many similar meals since he was...well, Nathan's age.

His thoughts turning again to the little boy who surely had to be his son, Simon finally understood the urgency and the anger he'd heard in his parents' voices when they'd finally caught up with him two days ago. They must have only just realized themselves that the orphaned child left in Kit Davenport's care was his son, their grandson.

And when they did, they must have assumed, as Kit so obviously had, that he had not only left Belle, but also stayed away the past three years, to avoid his responsibility to Lucy and their baby.

But that wasn't true at all. He would have never abandoned Lucy or his child. He had fancied himself in love with her back then, and though he had since realized he'd been more infatuated with her freedom of spirit than anything else, he would have gladly married her.

She was the one who had ended their relationship, and she had done so in a way guaranteed to drive him out of her life for good.

But why had she treated him so hurtfully? Simon wondered. *Had* she been sexually intimate with another man? *Had* she really believed that he—Simon—wasn't the father of her child?

He wouldn't have thought she'd had the time or energy to fit another man into her life three years ago. They had been together every spare minute they'd had that summer. Kit Davenport, Lucy's best friend, had spent a lot of time with them, too.

Kit and Lucy had been extremely close, sharing all sorts of intimate secrets. And if Kit's hostility toward him in the diner was any indication, then she had been led to believe that he'd known he was Nathan's father all along—

A sharp *rap, rap, rap* against the SUV's driver's-side window startled Simon out of his reverie. Turning, he saw Winifred Averill staring at him, an accusatory look in her eyes as the morning breeze ruffled her mop of frizzy iron-gray curls.

Just what he needed—a lecture from one of Belle's oldest and most revered senior citizens, he thought as he rolled down the window. He had always admired the elderly woman's independence, and he had often been amused by her outrageous behavior. But at that particular moment, he would have preferred not to be the focus of her unabashed attention.

Since he didn't seem to have any choice in the matter, though, Simon met her gaze with a gracious smile. He had no reason to act as if he'd done anything wrong because he most certainly hadn't.

"Good morning, Mrs. Averill. It's nice to see you again. Weren't you having breakfast in the diner earlier?" he asked politely.

"Good morning to you, too, young man, and yes, I was having breakfast in the diner earlier," she acknowledged, though her tone was anything but friendly. "As for the pleasure of seeing *you* again, that's yet to be determined. By my reckoning, you've been less than dutiful the past few years."

He shouldn't be surprised that Winifred Averill assumed the worst about him. The tone of his last conversation with his parents indicated that they had, as well. Yet he couldn't recall doing anything in the past that would have made it so easy for people, especially those who should have known him best, to convict him without even hearing his side of the story.

Simon had never been intentionally cruel or neglectful in his life. But somehow he'd been painted as the villain where Lucy Kane was concerned. For the life of him, he couldn't begin to understand why.

"I guess it wouldn't cut any ice with you if I said that I only just found out about that little boy in the diner," he replied, trying not to sound as defensive as he had begun to feel.

Winifred held his gaze for several long, silent seconds. Then she gave a nod of seeming satisfaction.

"Most anybody else told me that, I'd say likely story. But you always struck me as a decent young man, Simon Gilmore, and you surely come from decent folks. Lucy Kane never pointed a finger at you publicly. I doubt people would have been any the wiser if that child's resemblance to you hadn't become so obvious lately. You're here now and you seem aware of your responsibilities. I imagine you'll do right by the youngster and by Miss Kit, as well. I believe that's what really matters."

"I'll certainly do my best, Mrs. Averill," he assured her, though he wasn't certain exactly how to begin.

Seeming to read his mind, Mrs. Averill tipped her head in the general direction of the diner, a few doors down the street from where Simon had parked his SUV.

"Might be wise of you to smooth Miss Kit's ruffled feathers," the elderly woman suggested. "She's had a lot to deal with the past six months. First her mother got sick. Poor Dolores only lasted a few weeks before the cancer took her in December. Then Lucy Kane ran her silly self into a tree, and Miss Kit took on the boy. She's been trying to sell the diner so she can go back to school in Seattle, but she hasn't had any takers. I'd say she could use a strong shoulder to lean on right about now."

"I hadn't heard about Mrs. Davenport," Simon said.

He understood even more how callous his behavior must have seemed to Kit. What had he been thinking, strolling up to her and kissing her the way he had?

That he'd been truly glad to see her just as he'd said....

"Not surprising with your folks gone as much as they are, but I'd head south for the winter if I could, too." Mrs. Averill nodded agreeably, then tapped a bony finger on Simon's arm. "You go on back to the Dinner Belle and talk to Kit. Take a few minutes and get to know that little boy of yours, too. He's a fine one, if I do say so myself—just like his daddy, too," she added, favoring him with a knowing smile before she headed off down the sidewalk to her rusty old pickup truck parked in front of the post office.

Daddy....

Overwhelmed yet again by the new reality he faced, Simon slowly rolled up the window and took his key from the ignition. He would take Mrs. Averill's advice and talk to Kit again before he drove out to the ranch. He was going to have a lot of explaining to do when he finally saw his parents, and he wanted to be able to give them straight answers to the questions he had no doubt they were going to ask.

If anybody could tell him what he needed to know about Lucy and Nathan, it had to be Kit Davenport. Getting past her anger and hostility would be a challenge, but one he was ready to face. He hadn't been able to think straight earlier. But he was ready now to present his case to her in a calm and deliberate manner.

With an odd sense of anticipation—all things considered—Simon walked the short distance back to the diner, savoring as best he could the lovely day. The sun had begun to warm with the first taste of summer heat, in counterpoint to the still-crisp, cool air coming off the snow-covered mountains of Glacier National Park, reminding him of how much he'd longed for just such days after the long frozen winters of his childhood.

He hadn't minded trading months of ice, snow and sub-zero temperatures for the mist and drizzle of Seattle…until now. He had forgotten how invigorating late spring and early summer could be in this quiet town he'd once called home. But he would remember now, and come back more often. In fact, his parents would insist on it so they could see their grandson.

Having no doubts at all that Mitchell and Deanna would welcome the new addition to their family with open arms, Simon strode into the Dinner Belle Diner with renewed confidence in his mission. He was more determined than ever to sort things out with Kit. He would let her know, too, that he'd be making arrangements to take over

Nathan's care. He didn't want her to be overburdened any longer.

Fewer people remained in the diner than when he'd first stopped by, and none gave him more than a cursory glance as he walked through the door again. He saw immediately that the playpen was empty. Kit no longer stood behind the counter, either, but Simon fully expected the ding of the bell above the door to bring her out of the kitchen. Instead, a slightly older woman bustled into the dining room to greet him, her blond hair bouncing around her shoulders.

Simon recognized her after a moment as the diner's longtime part-time waitress, and met her startled look with a slightly sheepish smile.

"Hey, Bonnie Lennox, good to see you again." He greeted her in his most cordial tone.

Seeming unable to help herself, Bonnie smiled, too, as she paused by the counter.

"Well, hey to you, too, Simon Gilmore. I thought I saw you sitting outside in that fancy black SUV parked at the curb a few doors down the street. What brings you to the Dinner Belle Diner?"

Though her tone was friendly, as well, the look Bonnie gave him was weighted heavily with reserve.

"Back to the Dinner Belle Diner, actually. I was here a little earlier as you may have heard from Kit," he said, testing the waters.

"She did mention that you'd stopped by," Bonnie admitted, her face flushing slightly at being caught out.

"Unfortunately, we didn't get off to a good start, and then I bolted like a scared rabbit. Finally got my head together, though." He allowed his smile to widen encouragingly. "Could you let her know that I'd really like to talk to her again if she's not too busy?"

"Well, I'm not sure that's possible." Bonnie hesitated, hands clasped at her waist. She looked as uncomfortable as she sounded. "We're a little shorthanded today and folks are going to be coming for lunch real soon—"

"It's okay, Bonnie, I'll talk to him," Kit said, appearing suddenly in the kitchen doorway, holding Nathan in her arms. "George is here now. He can finish up the lunch prep."

Simon had suspected that Kit had been lurking just out of sight in the kitchen, and he couldn't blame her for it. Now eyeing her openly as she spoke to Bonnie, he tried to measure how receptive she might be.

She hadn't changed a lot in the years since he'd last seen her, but she had changed in ways that were definitely distinctive. She had cut off her mouse-brown, shoulder-length hair, highlighted it with threads of honey-blond and now wore it sensibly short and fashionably spiked. No longer hidden by a heavy fall of hair, her fragile features stood out in a striking way. Her wide green eyes, especially, were lovelier than he remembered. She had never been plain, but now she was truly pretty. She seemed much more confident, but also, understandably, much less light-hearted.

"We can talk upstairs, although I'm not really sure it's necessary."

With all-too-obvious reluctance, Kit finally met Simon's gaze, the look she gave him one of grudging tolerance. Then she headed toward the staircase that led up to the apartment above the diner where she had lived with her mother.

Simon had been up there a few times in the past, but always with Lucy, never on his own.

"Oh, I'd say it was necessary," he said.

He understood and accepted her suspicion of him. But he meant her no harm, as he intended to prove to her soon enough. He was there to help her, not hurt her.

"I can't imagine why." She ducked her head as she led the way up the creaking wooden steps.

"Don't be coy, Kit. It doesn't become you," he advised, suddenly tired of sparring with her verbally.

"I'm not—" she protested.

"You are," Simon stated unequivocally. Then, his gaze now on Nathan, peeping over Kit's shoulder at him with bright, inquisitive eyes, he added, "But just so you know for sure, I'm here because of Nathan. He's my son and I've come to collect him."

Already halfway up the steps, Kit faltered as he spoke. Luckily he was able to catch her as she stumbled and save her from a bad fall. Hands on her forearms, he steadied her gently as she tried to regain her balance. The look she gave him—glancing back at him—held more hostility than gratitude. But still, combined with the feel of her warm, soft, bare skin against the palms of his hands, it sent an unexpected jolt zinging through him.

Reflexively he tightened his grip on her, the urge to pull her closer seeming to come out of nowhere almost more than he could resist—just as the urge to kiss her had been earlier. Contrarily Kit responded by jerking free of his grasp with something akin to a snarl. Then she continued up the steps without another word or another glance in his direction.

His male ego slightly bruised from her prickly retreat, Simon trailed after her, trying to keep his overactive libido in check. Good thing she'd had sense enough to shrug him off or he would have likely done something stupid. He had no idea what had come over him, but he had to be crazy to even consider hitting on Kit Davenport, especially under the circumstances. Yet for the time it took him to reach the top of the stairs, his eyes glued to her slender derriere, Simon Gilmore could think of little else.

Only when they were face-to-face again in the living room of the modestly furnished apartment, and Nathan gurgled and waved his teddy bear at him in seeming invitation, did Simon give himself a firm mental shake.

He wasn't there for Kit. He was there for his son, and it was time to let her know it in no uncertain terms.

Chapter Three

Kit had anticipated that Simon would return to the Dinner Belle Diner. She just hadn't expected to see him again quite so soon. Since he hadn't come back immediately after their initial confrontation, she had thought she'd have at least a day or two to marshal her resources before he showed his face at the Dinner Belle again. In fact, she had counted on at least having a chance to talk to Isaac Woodrow, the local attorney who was working with her to finalize Nathan's adoption.

Kit had been sure that Isaac would be able to calm her fears regarding Simon and any rights he might choose to claim. Because Simon couldn't possibly have *any* rights at all where Nathan was concerned—not to Kit's way of thinking, at least—and certainly not at this late date.

He had heartlessly abandoned Lucy during her pregnancy even though he'd known she was carrying his child. And he hadn't done anything since then to indicate that he'd given his own child the slightest bit of thought. Then he'd popped back into town and strolled into the diner, cocky as could be, ready to be welcomed home like a hero rather than the cowardly jerk he'd proven himself to be.

As if, Kit had thought, wanting to scrub the taste of his kiss from her lips.

He'd fled fast enough when confronted with proof of his irresponsibility—no big surprise there. But now he was back again, ready to talk to her. That was just fine and dandy with her. She had a lot to say to him, none of it good, and she knew she'd feel better once she'd gotten the bulk of the ill will she felt toward him off her chest.

Convinced that she had the upper hand, Kit had felt comfortable enough inviting Simon into her home. She'd been too smug, too soon, though, as she'd quickly discovered.

Climbing the staircase to the apartment, following along behind her in seeming docility, Simon Gilmore had neatly turned the tables on her. He had spouted absolute nonsense about *collecting* his son, as if Nathan were a parcel he'd forgotten at the post office. He had scared her so badly, she'd teetered on the wooden steps. And though he had caught her easily, saving her from a fall, his consideration offered her no reassurance at all.

Instead, the touch of Simon's hands on her had triggered something even more frightening deep inside of her.

For the space of several heartbeats, Kit Davenport had been tempted to lean on Simon Gilmore. She'd had to be so strong for so long all on her own. She had nursed her mother through a terminal illness, and at the same time, she had managed to keep the Dinner Belle Diner open for business. Then she had taken on full responsibility for an orphaned toddler she truly loved.

The lure of Simon's masculine strength—offered with seeming kindness and solicitude—had been almost more than she could resist. How easy she had found it in those few moments to believe that he meant her no harm. She had thought of him as a friend once, he had seemed to remind her. He could be her friend again if only she would let him.

But then Kit had remembered that he'd been no friend to Lucy, and wouldn't be to her, either. Not as long as he thought he had the right to take Nathan away from her. Lucy had taken special care to name *her* as the little boy's guardian. Surely that, alone, would negate any claim Simon attempted to make, and surely her attorney would agree.

Maybe she should tell Simon she'd rather not talk to him, after all. Maybe she should confer with Isaac first just to be certain of her rights. Better yet, maybe she should send Simon to see Isaac. As a family law attorney in practice for many years, Isaac Woodrow would know a lot more about her legal standing than she. He could speak not only with knowledge but also authority, and he could make sure Simon didn't harass her in any way during the time he remained in Belle.

Having regained her confidence, Kit turned to face Simon as he closed the apartment door. She was fully prepared to ask him to leave, but the look he directed her way in the instant before Nathan distracted him was so resolute that her breath caught in her throat. He was a man with a mission, and he wouldn't be easily deflected. Short of causing a scene that would embarrass them both, she doubted she'd be able to get rid of him until he, personally, was ready to go.

Talking to him would cost her little more than time, and she might even gain some peace of mind. Altruistic as he now seemed, Simon couldn't possibly know all that was involved in raising a child. Once he realized how much time, energy and emotion good parenting required, odds were he'd bow out just like he had three years ago.

She would only pitch a fit if Simon tried to take Nathan away from her, Kit decided. Bonnie and George were close by. They would come to her rescue if need be.

Though watching Simon's expression soften as he gazed at Nathan, Kit couldn't believe he'd ever threaten her or harm her physically. He had always been a patient man. He had also treated everyone he knew with kindness and understanding—including Lucy, even when her behavior toward him had been careless and chaotic.

Running out on her, as he had the one time she'd really needed him, had seemed totally out of character to Kit. But the fact remained that he had—proof, as far as Kit was concerned, that he wasn't nearly as good or kind or decent as she'd once believed him to be.

"It's time for Nathan to have his lunch," Kit said, maintaining a pragmatic tone, but only with great effort. "Why don't you join us in the kitchen? We can talk while I feed him."

Simon seemed to fill the apartment's cozy living room with his masculine presence. Though nicely furnished and quite comfortable under normal circumstances, it certainly wasn't spacious. At least not spacious enough for a woman, namely her, who would have rather not been in close quarters with a man, namely Simon, whom she considered more of an enemy than friend.

Unfortunately, the kitchen was smaller still. Kit's

mother had rarely used it, preferring, as she had, to cook in the diner's larger and better-equipped facility. Kit didn't cook there, either. She mostly just reheated whatever leftovers she brought up from the diner for herself and Nathan.

Giving the little boy his meals in the upstairs kitchen had become a part of their routine, though—one that Kit was loathe to disrupt. She had learned that any change in routine tended to make Nathan extremely fussy. Not unusual, considering he'd lost his mother, and certainly understandable. Upsetting him in order to keep Simon at a distance that would be nominal at best simply wasn't necessary.

"Can I do anything to help?" Simon asked, following her as she headed for the kitchen doorway.

"I'm used to managing on my own," she answered in a tart tone, bristling at him all over again before she could stop herself.

She didn't like feeling crowded on any front, and just then Simon seemed to loom large—his broad shoulders and powerful physique making her feel ill at ease. He wasn't being obnoxious about it, and he'd meant well, offering to help, but still…

"Of course, you are," he said, pausing just inside the kitchen doorway, obviously aware of her discomfort. "I just thought you might be glad to have someone lend a hand for a change. But I'll stay out of your way if that's what you'd prefer."

She was making a difficult situation even more so by behaving in such a disdainful manner, Kit thought, drawing a calming breath as she settled Nathan into his high chair and fastened the safety straps. Simon was right. She regularly wished she had someone to help her.

"You can get one of the bottles out of the refrigerator and put it in the bottle warmer on the counter to heat up," she said, her tone now slightly conciliatory.

"So he still takes a bottle?"

Simon seemed genuinely interested as he followed her instructions without any fumbling or bumbling.

"Only after he's eaten lunch. It helps him settle down for a nap. He gave up his bedtime bottle about six weeks ago. He decided one night that he didn't want it."

Moving efficiently around the tiny kitchen, managing somehow not to bump into Simon, Kit took a container of chicken noodle soup out of the refrigerator, dumped it into a pan on the stove and lit the burner. She gave Nathan a cracker to tide him over, opened a fresh jar of apple juice and poured some into a sippy cup. He reached for it eagerly, babbling in a happy voice.

"He seems like a good baby," Simon ventured, stirring the soup with the spoon she'd left in the pot.

Very domestic, she acknowledged to herself, stepping around him to get a bowl from one of the cabinets above the counter. He had only taken a few seconds to figure out how to work the bottle warmer, too. He certainly deserved an A for effort, but that didn't change the fact that he'd treated her best friend like dirt.

Reminded that she owed Simon no appreciation at all, Kit reached up to open the cabinet, and much to her chagrin, brushed against him accidentally. The physical contact, slight as it was, sent a shaft of heat through her. Startled, she almost dropped the bowl as she spun away from him.

Seeming equally off-kilter, Simon winced and shifted to the side, away from her, as well. Embarrassed, Kit plunked the bowl on the counter and turned to take a spoon from the drawer by the sink.

"He's very good…all things considered," she said, not really caring that she sounded snappish again.

Kit could feel Simon's gaze on her as he continued to stir the soup. She could also sense that he was eyeing her with renewed frustration. Better that than getting too comfortable around her, she thought. It wasn't her responsibility or her intention to make the present situation easy for him. He hadn't earned easy from her, and as far as she was concerned, he never would, no matter how her body betrayed her with girlish longing.

The young man she'd secretly desired years ago had proven to have feet of clay. He had used Lucy, then abandoned her, and he would probably do the same to her if she gave him half a chance.

"Looks like the soup is ready," he said. "Do you want me to spoon some of it into the bowl?"

"Yes, please."

Kit stood by in silence as Simon carefully filled the bowl halfway. Then she picked it up off the counter and carried to the table. She sipped a spoonful, testing to make sure it wasn't too hot, then offered some to Nathan. Sitting with her back to Simon, she tried to pretend he wasn't there. Finally he moved to the chair across from her and sat down with an audible sigh.

"I didn't know Lucy was pregnant with my child," he said, his voice low but steady, commanding her attention with his simply spoken, and utterly unbelievable, statement.

Kit's first instinct was to lash out at him in anger. He had a lot of nerve saying such a thing to her. He couldn't

honestly think he'd gain ground with her by spouting such
a ridiculous lie. She wasn't stupid, after all, and she'd been
Lucy's best friend. There had been no secrets between
them—not where Simon Gilmore was concerned.

Remembering how upset Nathan had been the few
times Lucy raised her voice in front of him, Kit managed
to keep her emotions in check, however. There was no need
to throw a tempter tantrum and cause the child to cry. Not
when she could make her point just as forcefully in a calm,
quiet manner.

"Give me a break, Simon," she said, her voice low, as
well, but heavily laced with sarcasm. "You knew Lucy
was pregnant when you left Belle three years ago. She told
you about the baby the last time you were together, and
you took off like a shot the very next day. You abandoned
her and you abandoned your child and you didn't give either of them a second thought. Don't come around here
now, trying to change history. It's not going to work—at
least not with me."

"I'm not trying to change history, Kit," Simon insisted.

Sitting forward in his chair, his hands gripping the edge
of the oak table, he seemed unwilling to let the matter drop.
Kit bit back another caustic comment with a grim twist of
her lips, and glanced at him with exasperation, her look all
but shouting "Oh, please."

"I'm not," he said again, his voice suddenly turning
hard and cold as steel. "It's true Lucy told me she was pregnant the last time I saw her, and I did leave town the next
day. But there's something Lucy also told me that she evidently didn't bother to share with you. It's the real reason
why I left town the way I did, and the main reason I haven't
really wanted to return."

"Lucy and I didn't keep secrets from each other," Kit insisted, making no effort to hide her continued distrust of him. "We were best friends…always."

"I didn't think Lucy kept secrets from me, either, and we were a hell of a lot more than best friends. But I know now that she did."

"That doesn't mean she kept secrets from me, too," Kit shot back defensively.

"Just hear me out, okay?" Simon pleaded, his frustration evident though his voice was still low. "Then you can decide how honest Lucy Kane really was with us."

"Okay, fine. Say whatever it is you have to say. Just don't expect me to believe you," Kit advised.

With a negligent shrug of her shoulders, she turned her attention to feeding Nathan.

"The night Lucy told me she was pregnant she also told me the baby wasn't mine," Simon began, only the slightest bit hesitant. "She said she'd been seeing someone else over the summer, someone she said that she loved more than me. She also told me he was the one who had fathered her baby."

Kit stared at Simon then, unable to hide her surprise. Lucy—seeing someone else? Impossible—

"I didn't want to believe her, Kit," Simon continued insistently. "In fact, I *refused* to believe her until she looked me straight in the eye and said it all again, just as calm as you please. She told me to have a nice life in Seattle, then she gave me a little kiss on the cheek by way of goodbye. Talk about a kick in the teeth."

Simon's version of how he and Lucy had parted company was too outrageous to even be considered. Yet the look of anguish Kit saw in his eyes before he glanced away was so genuine that she couldn't dismiss what he'd told her. The thought came to her that he might just be telling her the truth, and with that thought came a cold rush of fear.

Lucy hadn't really wanted to go with Simon to Seattle. She had admitted as much to Kit more than once that summer. But would she have lied to him about her pregnancy so she wouldn't have to? Though Kit didn't want to think her friend could have been so cruel or so deceptive, Simon's revelation had set off a tremor of uncertainty that was already beginning to shake her faith in her friend.

"Yeah, I left Belle, Montana, in a rush, all right," Simon added in a musing tone when Kit made no comment. Sitting back in his chair, he crossed his arms over his chest defensively. "I couldn't get away from here fast enough. I wouldn't have come back now except my parents called and told me I had some *family business* that needed tending. They didn't give me any details, but I'm guessing they've been thinking what you and half the town must have been thinking of me lately. Only it's not true, Kit. I didn't intentionally abandon Lucy or my child. That's not the kind of man I am, and you, of all people, should know it."

Mechanically, Kit finished feeding Nathan his soup, saying nothing though her thoughts whirled a mile a minute.

She was no longer convinced that Simon was lying to her. He'd told his side of the story with too much sincerity for her to dismiss it as a fabrication. There was also no reason for him to go to so much trouble offering excuses. No one had asked him to take responsibility for Nathan's welfare.

Well, she hadn't, and she wouldn't in the future, but maybe his parents would. Only it wasn't going to be necessary. Once the adoption was final, Nathan would be her child, legally, and she was more than capable of caring for him all on her own.

Finally Kit glanced at Simon again as she helped Nathan take another drink from his cup. He eyed her stubbornly in return, still waiting for her to respond. She wasn't sure what to say to him. The *truth* Lucy had told *her* was so different from *his* truth. Maybe it warranted repeating.

"Lucy told *me* that you knew the baby was yours. She told *me* that's why you left town. She said you didn't want to be tied down to a wife and family. She bawled like a baby when she told me you'd gone, and she was miserable for a long time after you left." Pausing, Kit frowned and looked away again. "It's unlikely she was seeing someone else—highly unlikely. She was either with you or me or both of us that summer, and she was working at the diner, too. She wouldn't have had time to fit in a secret lover, and if she had, I'm sure she would have told me. We were so close…."

"I thought we were close, too, Lucy and I, but obviously I was wrong," Simon said. "She lied to me, Kit, and she lied to you, too. You can either admit it to yourself, or not, but that's the one basic truth in the whole damned mess she created."

"But why?" Kit demanded fiercely, suddenly more afraid than ever. "Why did she lie to us? She must have had some good reason."

If Simon was right about Lucy—if she intentionally kept him from his son—then he might actually have a legitimate claim to Nathan. He had already said he wanted his son. But he couldn't just take him away from her. She was already his legal guardian and the adoption was very near to being finalized—

"I don't know why," Simon admitted. "I've been trying to figure it out since I first saw Nathan standing in his playpen. She knew I loved her and she knew I wanted her to live with me in Seattle. Hell, I must have asked her to marry me half a dozen times that summer. She'd just smile and say she'd think about it.

"Then she said the one thing she had to know was guaranteed to run me off. You were her best friend, Kit. You were the one she would have trusted most, yet she lied to you, too, didn't she?"

"Only if I believe what *you've* told me is the truth," Kit countered.

Gathering Nathan's empty bowl and cup, she pushed away from the table and crossed to the sink, turning her back on Simon. He was making too much sense for her peace of mind.

"Why would I lie to you?" Simon asked relentlessly, echoing the question she'd posed to herself once already.

"So you can strut around town again without looking like a jerk," she retorted, aware that she was grasping at straws.

Why would Simon Gilmore care what anyone in tiny Belle, Montana, thought of him—including her? He could certainly snow his own parents without a practice run, and he had a whole other life in Seattle, Washington. None of his friends in the big city need ever know about his youthful indiscretion.

"You should know me better than that after all the time we spent together, Kit," Simon chided her gently. "I've made my share of mistakes and I've always owned up to them. But I'm not hanging my head in shame over something I didn't do. And I did *not* abandon Lucy or my son."

"I thought I knew Lucy, too, but now I'm not so sure," Kit admitted, failing to realize until too late that she had finally sided with him, at least in an indirect way.

"That's not exactly a vote of total confidence, but hey, I'll take what I can get," Simon said, his gruff tone lightening perceptively. Then as Kit took Nathan's bottle from the warmer, he added to the little boy, "Hey, buddy, how about I get you out of that high chair?"

Clutching the baby bottle in both hands, Kit spun around to face Simon again, just as he lifted Nathan into his arms. The child went to him willingly, looking up at him with wondering eyes. His expression grave but unafraid, Nathan patted Simon's jaw with one little hand. Simon seemed equally enchanted by his son, returning the little boy's gaze with one full of awe.

Kit was both endeared and terrified by the sight of father and son taking their first tentative steps in the bonding process. Simon couldn't think she'd let him take Nathan away from her on the basis of some wild, impossible-to-prove story.

"Let me have him," she demanded.

Her voice sounding harsh and afraid to her ears as she plunked the bottle on the table, she reached for Nathan.

Obviously startled by her tone, Simon took a step back. His hold on Nathan seemed to tighten as he gazed at her in confusion. Nathan, too, stared at her, his eyes widening, his lower lip beginning to quiver.

Pain squeezed at Kit's heart as she thought of how easily Simon could turn and walk out of the apartment with

Nathan still in his arms. The way he was standing, he had a clear shot through the kitchen to the front door. She wasn't strong enough to stop him physically. She doubted George and Bonnie together would be, either, even if she managed to alert them in time.

Tears welled in her eyes and her hands began to shake. She couldn't lose Nathan. Not after all the other losses she'd suffered in the past six months.

"Please," she begged, unable to hide her desperation as she held her arms out to Simon in supplication. "Please let me have him…."

Chapter Four

Simon stared at Kit in silence for several long, confusing moments, unsure at first what had triggered the high note of panic in her voice as she reached out so greedily for Nathan. He had only been trying to lend a hand, wanting to release the fidgeting little boy from the confines of his high chair before he began to fuss.

Taking such action had seemed harmless enough, and of course he'd handled Nathan with consummate care. He had thought Kit would appreciate the help, busy as she was rinsing dishes at the sink, then fetching Nathan's bottle from the warmer. But the longing that had built steadily inside of him as he'd sat by the table, talking to Kit, had motivated him, as well.

Focusing more and more of his attention on the child happily eating the chicken soup and saltines she fed him so patiently, Simon had noted the many physical similarities between him and his son. He had seen in Nathan, too, something of Lucy in the determined tilt of his little chin and the elegant arch of his eyebrows.

With increasing urgency Simon had wanted to feel the warm, solid weight of his son's small body in his arms. He had needed to hold his child close, to look into his bright blue eyes with the gentle reassurance of a father promising his beloved child that he would move heaven and earth to make sure everything in his world would always be just fine.

Your daddy's here now, little guy, and he's going to take very good care of you.

Understanding finally dawned on Simon as Kit continued to stand in front of him, however, her eyes darkened by the shadow of inexpressible fear. She must have sensed the intensity of his determination to accept responsibility for the son he only now knew he had. And she must now think that he intended to take Nathan from her at that very moment.

No wonder she had panicked, Simon thought, his heart going out to her in sympathy. She must see him as her enemy, when that wasn't his intention at all. They had been friends once. For Nathan's sake, he hoped they could be friends again.

Kit had said that Lucy named her as the boy's legal guardian. She had also said that she was in the process of adopting him, and it was apparent, by all she'd said and done, that she loved and cherished him deeply.

In the months since Lucy's death Kit had mothered Nathan as if he were her own child. She was the one constant in his son's short life, and she was the one Nathan reached for now with a tearful whimper, aware as children always are, of emotions running high.

Simon knew that he would gain nothing by alienating Kit Davenport, and he would upset Nathan, as well, by behaving like a bully. There were ways that he could go about asserting his parental rights in a calm and dignified manner. He truly had no desire at all to cause Kit unnecessary pain.

To his way of thinking, he owed her an enormous debt of gratitude. Had it not been for her generosity of spirit, Nathan could have become a ward of the state. Put into a foster home and eventually adopted by strangers, his son would never have known he had a father ready and willing to love and care for him.

No, Simon didn't want to hurt Kit, or upset her unnecessarily. But he wasn't going to give up his son to her, either—at least not on any kind of permanent basis.

Of course, he was going to need time to bond with his son before he would be ready to take over as a full-time father. And Kit was the one person who could facilitate that bonding. Her acceptance of him would, in turn, guarantee Nathan's acceptance of him, and only with mutual acceptance and understanding would they avoid any further emotional trauma.

"Hey, no problem," Simon said finally, shifting Nathan into Kit's arms with a reassuring smile. "I hope I didn't scare him."

The little boy's quivering lip vanished as he snuggled contentedly against Kit's shoulder. Her relief was almost palpable as she held the child close. But there was also embarrassment evident in the lingering glance she shot Simon's way.

"Actually, I believe I'm the one who frightened him, raising my voice the way I did," she admitted, her slight smile rueful.

"You weren't afraid that I'd drop him or anything, were you?" Simon asked, wanting to find out just how honest she would be with him.

Kit hesitated a moment, her smile fading as she looked away, then met his gaze again, her chin tipped at a defensive angle.

"I trusted that you'd be careful with him," she said, her tone matter-of-fact. "What concerned me was the possibility that you'd try to leave with him, and I wouldn't be able to do anything to stop you."

Her truthfulness, coupled with her acknowledgment of just how vulnerable he'd made her feel, touched off deep in Simon's soul an unexpected inclination to protect. Had anyone posed a similar threat to Kit Davenport's well-being, he knew he would have come to her aid without a moment's hesitation. But the only way he could save her from himself was to give up his son, and that Simon could never do.

Again he realized how loathe he was to see Kit hurt, and again he admitted that he was the one most likely to cause her pain in the very near future. Unfortunately, he couldn't see that he had any choice in the matter. He could be as honest as she was, though, and hope that she would respect him for it as he respected her.

"The thought did cross my mind," he said. "Nathan *is* my son, after all.

"But there are other issues involved, legal issues that we'll have to sort out. There's also the fact that he doesn't know me very well yet. It's going to be a while before he's as comfortable with me as he is with you. If I'd taken off with him, I would have probably scared him half to death. That wouldn't do any of us any good, but especially wouldn't have been good for Nathan. His best interests have to come first, as I'm sure you'll agree."

"Of course, I agree that his best interests are of primary importance. But just because you happened to donate the sperm doesn't automatically give you parental rights," Kit retorted in righteous indignation, all evidence of weakness on her part gone in a flash. Holding Nathan tight, she squared her shoulders and met his gaze unswervingly. "I'm the one Lucy designated as *her* son's guardian. Nothing was said about *you* in her will. I don't think she would have left you out of the equation if she wanted you to be a part of Nathan's life."

"Lucy made a lot of decisions about *our* son that didn't include me," Simon pointed out, his own ire returning in full force. "But only because I didn't know I had a son, thanks to her deception. I know about Nathan now, though, and I'm not letting you exclude me the way she did. I'm a good man and I deserve to have the chance to raise my son. You can try to fight me if you want to, Kit. But be forewarned—while I don't want to see you hurt, I *will* do whatever it takes to get full custody of my son."

He spoke in a measured tone, never once raising his voice. Still Kit seemed to wilt under his barrage. She didn't respond verbally in any way, just looked at him with wide, suddenly frightened eyes. Despite all his justifications, spoken and unspoken, in that moment she made him feel like a bully. He could blame her for the provocation, but that didn't excuse completely his intimidating behavior.

"I want you with me, Kit, not against me," he added, softening his voice as he reached out to touch her cheek with gentle fingertips.

She flinched away from him as if she'd been scalded.

"It's Lucy's wishes that matter to me, not yours, Simon Gilmore. Lucy wanted me, not you, to take care of Nathan if anything happened to her, and that's exactly what I plan to do."

"Then I guess I'll see you in court," he stated simply, accepting at last that they'd reached an impasse.

"Yes, I guess you will."

He had said as much as he could, Simon thought, and probably more than he should. Turning away from Kit, he made his way to the door. He didn't like leaving after such an acrimonious exchange, but neither was he prepared to alter his stance or to take back anything he'd said.

He had tried to be reasonable as he'd stated his case, but Kit hadn't wanted to be reasonable in return. Now there seemed nothing left to do but head out to the ranch. He'd talk to his parents, and then he would hire an attorney to represent him.

There was no telling how long it would take to win custody of his son. But he had four weeks' time to get the process started, and he intended to go the distance no matter what it cost him in the end.

To Kit, the hollow sound of the apartment door closing had a frightening ring of finality about it. She wanted to go after Simon and rage at him in the worst way. But all she could do was stand in her tiny kitchen, holding Nathan in her arms, a sick twist in the pit of her stomach.

He had a lot of nerve showing up in Belle, claiming Lucy had lied to him three years ago, then sputtering angrily about *his* rights. He had likely expected she'd give in to his forcefulness. She was a woman alone, after all, with limited financial resources. But she'd stood her ground, and so he'd upped the ante, changing his tactics like a chameleon changes color.

He had caught her off guard, touching her the way he had so unexpectedly, his hand gentle against her face. For one long moment she had been tempted to believe that he wished her no harm—that when he said he wanted her with him, not against him, they *could* be partners for Nathan's benefit.

But then common sense had come to the fore. Simon wanted her cooperation only so that he could gain custody of his son without a legal battle. Once he'd accomplished that task, he'd have no need of her. She would be shuffled off to the sidelines, and eventually, as time passed, the child she'd come to love as her own would be lost to her forever.

The possibility that such a fate awaited her anyway loomed large in Kit's mind as she retrieved Nathan's bottle from the table where she'd set it earlier. Through the adoption process, she had learned a little about the laws regarding child custody. But not nearly enough, she admitted now, the dread that had made her stomach roil settling into her soul, as well.

She knew that biological parents had certain rights where their children were concerned unless they gave up those rights willingly or had them taken away by the court. Simon had made it clear that he wanted custody of his son, so he certainly wasn't going to give up his rights voluntarily. Unless he could be proven to be a danger to the child, the court wasn't likely to stand in his way, either.

But what about Lucy's rights, not to mention her wishes? Wouldn't a mother's say about who raised her child have some sway with a judge? And if not, where did that leave *her?* Kit wondered. She would have to call Isaac

Woodrow just as soon as she could. Surely he would be able to answer her questions and perhaps even calm her fears.

First things first, though, she told herself as she shifted her attention to the little boy she held in her arms. Ready for his bottle and afternoon nap, Nathan had begun to squirm and fuss impatiently while she let her fears get the better of her. She would be no good to herself or Nathan or to Lucy's memory if she adopted a defeatist attitude before she had all the facts of the matter.

"Come on, kiddo. Let's get you settled," Kit said, glancing at the clock in the kitchen, then heading for the kitchen doorway.

Amazingly it wasn't quite eleven-thirty. She shouldn't be surprised since Sara Hale, the college student who looked after Nathan from eleven-thirty till three, hadn't arrived yet and she was always on time. Still, to Kit, it seemed impossible that so little time had passed considering how completely her life had been changed since Simon had first strolled into the Dinner Belle Diner that morning.

The biggest worry she'd had to face when her alarm had sounded at dawn had been finding a buyer for the diner. Now that seemed like hardly any problem at all, faced as she suddenly was with the possibility of losing Nathan.

Aware that she'd have an easier time slipping back down to the diner if Nathan was asleep when Sara arrived, Kit made fast work of changing the little boy's diaper and tucking him into his bed with his bottle. He gazed at her with sleepy eyes and smiled at her for an instant, his little mouth curving around the bottle's nipple in a way that made her heart ache.

Gripping the bed rail with both hands, she stood over

him until he let go of the bottle and drifted off to sleep. She reached out to take the bottle with one hand and, with the other, she gently smoothed his dark curls from his forehead.

As her fingers grazed the downy softness of the child's skin, Kit thought again of how Simon had touched *her,* but in another, less defensive, light. She had been shocked and appalled by the familiar way in which he'd kissed her. But they *had* been friends once, and if what he'd said about Lucy was true, he would have had no reason to expect anything but a warm welcome from her.

She'd been startled by his tenderness when he'd caught her on the staircase, as well, especially coming as it had on the heels of his rant about fatherly rights. But looking back on the moment, she couldn't reject the caring and concern he'd shown her as being insincere.

She had seen the candor in his eyes and heard it in his voice as he'd said that he wanted her with him, and she had responded, if only for an instant, in a way that had frightened her then, and now. She had been alone so long, facing one tragedy after another—her mother's illness, then her death and then Lucy's death. How easy it would be to lean on him, just as she had done when she'd stumbled on the steps and he'd saved her from a fall. How easy it had been to trust in the promise of benevolence he'd held out to her then.

Kit had never thought of Simon Gilmore as a hurtful person until he'd abandoned Lucy. And if he hadn't run out on his responsibilities as Lucy had claimed—if, in fact, Lucy had lied to him as well to her—then she had no reason to think of him as a hurtful person now.

Only, he'd said he was going to take Nathan away from her. There was no more hurtful thing he could do to her.

A soft tap on the front door announced Sara's arrival. Time to put Simon out of her mind—ditto the havoc he could cause, Kit thought. Tables had likely begun to fill in the diner and much as she wanted to call Isaac immediately, she knew her help would be needed there until the crowd dwindled.

Reluctantly Kit left Nathan sleeping in his bed and hurried to answer the door, managing somehow to dredge up à smile for sweet, young Sara somewhere along the way.

"You didn't tell me that you knew the identity of Nathan's father," Isaac Woodrow said, his tone slightly accusatory.

"You didn't ask," Kit answered, trying not to sound as defensive as she felt.

She had called Isaac as planned after the diner's 3:30 p.m. closing time, and had explained the situation to him as calmly as she could. He'd listened without comment until she'd finished. But then, instead of offering her the reassurance she'd needed, her lawyer·had made her sound like the culpable party.

"I assumed Ms. Kane wasn't sure who the father was since she didn't list a name on the child's birth certificate."

"I didn't think it mattered who Nathan's father was since Lucy named me as his guardian. She obviously didn't want Simon Gilmore to have him. I had to agree with her because of the way he abandoned her."

"But you're saying now that Mr. Gilmore is claiming Ms. Kane told him he wasn't the father of her child. That would preclude any attempt at accusing him of abandonment."

"Maybe Lucy had a reason why she didn't want Simon

involved in Nathan's upbringing. Maybe he behaved badly toward her," Kit insisted, though she admitted to herself that it was highly unlikely.

"That would have to be proven, Ms. Davenport."

"He could be lying about what Lucy told him," she said, returning to her original argument. "So it would be his word against mine, wouldn't it?"

"Regardless of what occurred between Mr. Gilmore and Ms. Kane three years ago, if Mr. Gilmore *is* the child's biological father and *if* he wants custody of the child, then the court will give his claim serious consideration," Isaac explained patiently. "And to be perfectly frank, unless he can be proven to be a danger to the child, his rights will most certainly take precedence over yours."

"How can that be possible? I'm his legal guardian," Kit pointed out, unwilling to just give up.

"I'm sorry, Ms. Davenport, but it's the law. Be grateful he's shown up now instead of two years from now when the transition for Nathan would be even more difficult. But we're getting ahead of ourselves here with worst-case scenarios. Mr. Gilmore may actually be willing to give up his rights once he's considered all that's involved in becoming a single parent. He was understandably angry about what he believes to be Ms. Kane's deception, and he reacted accordingly. Given a little time to think about what he'd be taking on, perhaps he'll change his mind. Did he say he'd be hiring an attorney?"

"Not in so many words, but he did say he'd see me in court," Kit replied, tears of frustration stinging her eyes.

It was easy for Isaac to dismiss worst-case scenarios. He hadn't seen the determined look in Simon's eyes.

"Then let's give it a few days and see what develops."

"But the adoption is so close to being final. Isn't there some way you can get the judge to sign the papers?

"Not unless Mr. Gilmore agrees to give up his parental rights."

"But Lucy wanted *me* to take care of Nathan...."

"Again, I'm sorry, Ms. Davenport. We have to abide by the law in cases like this, and the law gives Mr. Gilmore certain rights regarding his son. I *will* do everything I can on your behalf, though. Under the circumstances, I'm sure I'll be able to arrange visitation for you at the very least, unless you choose to be openly hostile toward Mr. Gilmore. That certainly wouldn't work in your favor."

"Visitation?"

"I'm sure I'll be hearing from Mr. Gilmore's attorney in a few days. We'll talk again after that, all right?"

"Yes, of course...we can talk again."

Only Kit didn't want to talk to Isaac Woodrow anymore. She wanted to pack up all of her belongings, strap Nathan into his car seat and head out of Belle as fast as her aging car would go.

How could he think she'd be satisfied with visitation? Lucy had wanted Kit to take care of Nathan 24/7, not just see him occasionally at Simon Gilmore's convenience. As for curbing her hostility toward him...well, that just wasn't going to be possible.

Sadly, neither was making a run for it. Life on the lam would be no life for her or for Nathan. For one thing, they'd have no peace. Simon would be hot on their trail. She'd only be postponing the inevitable until he finally caught up with her. She might have Nathan with her for a little longer, but she would lose him eventually.

Better to stand and fight than run and hide, she told herself, brushing the tears from her cheeks with shaky hands. Then maybe all wouldn't be lost completely.

Chapter Five

Sitting in Isaac Woodrow's office the following after-noon, nervously smoothing a hand over the fabric of her khaki skirt, Kit mentally replayed the conversation she'd had with him the previous day. He hadn't given her much to hang on to in the way of hope. And she'd lost her grasp completely on the tiny threads she'd clung to during a long and sleepless night when he'd walked into the diner that morning, a grim look on his weathered face.

An attorney with a law firm in Helena, Montana, had contacted him on Simon Gilmore's behalf, Isaac explained. A meeting of the parties involved in the Nathan Kane mat-ter had been requested, and if Kit was agreeable, Isaac would let Simon's attorney know that she would be avail-able at three-thirty that afternoon, as suggested.

Kit hadn't been sure if she was more relieved or angry that Simon had acted so quickly. She'd been snappish with George and Bonnie after Isaac had gone, and curt with the customers she'd served, many of whom eyed her with un-spoken sympathy. But by the time she'd headed for Isaac's office, leaving Sara to look after Nathan, an odd sense of calm had settled over her.

Kit had been the first to arrive and had been promptly ushered into Isaac's inner sanctum by his legal assistant, who also happened to be his wife of forty-something years. Margie Woodrow's gaze held sympathy, too. But her manner was also brisk and businesslike enough to allow Kit to maintain at least a little of her dignity.

Isaac had just begun to say that Simon's attorney had an excellent reputation—that, in fact, he was experienced in all matters related to family law and was known to be extremely fair-minded—when the intercom buzzed and Margie announced their arrival.

Kit's heartbeat accelerated as the door opened, but she didn't turn immediately to acknowledge Simon or his attorney when Isaac stood to greet them. She kept her gaze on Isaac and noted the exact moment he realized how little doubt there could be that Simon Gilmore was Nathan Kane's biological father.

Isaac and his wife hadn't always lived in Belle. They'd moved to the small town from Missoula only two years earlier as a first step in his retirement from the full-time practice of family law. And while Isaac had likely met Mitchell and Deanna Gilmore at one time or another in the past two years, he wouldn't have had the opportunity to meet their son and see Nathan's striking resemblance to him, until now.

Isaac's gaze shifted to Kit for a long moment and she sensed in his look the same accusation she'd heard in his voice the previous afternoon. Again she wanted to defend herself. She hadn't intentionally misled him about the identity of Nathan's father. She had simply assumed that revealing Simon's relationship to the child wasn't necessary under the circumstances. She had no opportunity, though.

Isaac offered his hand first to Simon, then his attorney, John Mahoney, his frown changing almost instantly into a welcoming smile. Then he gestured to Kit, including her in the introductions with a look of beneficence.

"Mr. Mahoney, my client, Kit Davenport. Mr. Gilmore, I believe you and Ms. Davenport know each other already?"

Forced to greet Simon and his attorney, Kit turned reluctantly in her chair and gazed up at the two men, her own expression grim. No sense pretending that she was happy about the situation. No sense, either, pretending that they could be friends as Isaac seemed to indicate.

"Mr. Mahoney," she said, acknowledging the attorney first by offering him her hand.

"Ms. Davenport, it's nice to meet you."

John Mahoney appeared to be younger than Isaac was, though not by too many years, and unlike Isaac, who favored casual slacks and polo shirts, he was dressed in a gray suit, white shirt and stiffly knotted burgundy-and-gray striped tie. He had kind eyes, though, and a firm grip and pleasant voice. As he shook her hand, Kit wanted to dislike him, but it was almost impossible. He seemed to her as decent and honest as her own attorney.

Reluctantly, Kit then looked at Simon. He, too, wore more formal attire—at least for him. His jeans were new and neatly pressed—ditto his chambray shirt. For the occasion, he'd also donned a navy blue blazer that emphasized the broadness of his shoulders, and a navy blue silk tie that added a touch of elegance to his appearance. He'd had his hair trimmed, as well, exchanging unkempt for ultratidy in an effort, she assumed, to increase his credibility.

Kit didn't offer to shake his hand as she had with his attorney. She hadn't intended even to meet his gaze. But she couldn't ignore completely the intensity of his scrutiny.

Like two powerful magnets, his bright blue eyes seemed to rivet on her, demanding her attention. Cursing her weakness, she shifted her gaze by degrees—from a spot just over his shoulder, to the line of his jaw, to the soft fall of a curl on his forehead until, at last—

She drew a sharp breath as their gazes clashed and she saw in his eyes such a surfeit of emotions that her heart twisted with sudden compassion. There was pain and sadness, confusion and distrust, and a kind of questioning that seemed to ask of her both understanding and acceptance.

He, too, had spent a sleepless night, if the haggard look on his face was any indication. And he, too, seemed to be wondering how he'd ended up in that particular place at that particular time, facing off with someone he'd once thought of as a friend.

"Simon," she said at last, his name little more than a whisper on her lips.

Then, because she knew somewhere deep in her heart that he was a decent man worthy of her respect, and because, too, it seemed like the right thing to do, she held out her hand to him.

"Kit," he replied, his own voice soft as he gripped her hand with both of his and squeezed with gentle, reassuring strength. "Please...understand...."

She nodded once then withdrew from him, hating the unwelcome sting of tears in her eyes. She wanted more than anything to believe that he, not Lucy, had lied to her, and that he'd returned to Belle out of a sense of duty forced on him by his family.

But the boy she'd known years ago—the boy she'd watched become a man—had never been a liar or a cheat. And the man who stood before her now hadn't stepped forward to claim his son only out of obligation. He had stepped forward out of love for the son he'd only now discovered.

"Well, then, Mr. Mahoney, Mr. Gilmore, please sit down."

Isaac gestured to the two chairs positioned alongside hers in front of his desk. Simon's attorney prudently chose the one next to hers and Simon sat in the other.

"Would anyone like coffee, tea or a soft drink before we begin?" he added as he settled into his desk chair again.

After they had all declined politely, Isaac opened the file folder on his desk and sifted through the papers it held. Then he looked at each of them in turn.

"I assume we're all aware of the basic facts of the matter here. It's my understanding that Ms. Davenport and Mr. Gilmore discussed the situation regarding Nathan Kane— son of Lucy Kane, deceased—yesterday. It's also my understanding that Mr. Gilmore believes that he is the child's biological father, and he now intends to petition the court for custody of him."

Hearing Isaac's blunt statement delivered so pragmatically, Kit suddenly found it difficult to swallow. He made what seemed totally unreasonable sound acceptable. She wanted to protest, but she knew she couldn't do so calmly.

Aware that hysterics would do more to hurt than help her cause, she sat quietly, hands clasped tightly in her lap as John Mahoney agreed that, yes, those were the basic facts of the matter.

"I suggest that we start by establishing Mr. Gilmore's paternity of the child," Isaac continued. "I can see that there are obvious physical similarities between Mr. Gilmore and Nathan Kane, but to alleviate any possible doubt, I'm sure you will all agree that DNA testing should be done. I have the name and number of a reputable lab in Missoula that conducts such testing at a nominal fee, to be paid by Mr. Gilmore, of course, since he is the one attempting to establish his rights. The testing is noninvasive and should take no more than thirty minutes at the most. Results will be available within two to three weeks of the test date. They ask only that you call at least a day in advance so they can include you on their schedule of appointments."

"I'm assuming a court order won't be necessary for Ms. Davenport to cooperate with the testing of Nathan," Mr. Mahoney said.

Kit whipped around to glare at Simon's attorney angrily. How dare he suggest that *she* was a troublemaker bent on causing problems? He didn't even know her.

Of course, she had no idea what Simon might have said about her, especially after the *discussion* they'd had yesterday. But just because she'd stood up to him didn't mean she would go out of her way to thwart the legal process.

She shifted her gaze to Simon, but he seemed determined not to look at her. Her anger ratcheted up another notch as she drew a steadying breath, ready to defend herself against John Mahoney's false assumptions.

Seeming to sense her mood, Isaac hurried to speak on her behalf, his tone still matter-of-fact.

"I'm sure Ms. Davenport has no desire to drag this matter through the court system by initiating a lengthy legal battle. I'm sure, too, that she also understands, as we all do, that dealing with the issue of Nathan Kane's custody in a hostile and time-consuming manner would not be in the best interests of the child."

"Is that true, Ms. Davenport?" Mr. Mahoney asked, obviously wanting to hear her voice her own agreement.

"Yes, of course," she replied defensively. "I've always only wanted what's best for Nathan. I couldn't love him any more if I'd given birth to him. I feel as if he's my son now. I'd never do anything to hurt him—not intentionally."

She directed her avowal to John Mahoney, forcing herself to meet his gaze. But she knew that Simon had shifted his gaze to her, as well.

"Nathan Kane is *not* your child, though, Ms. Davenport," Mahoney pointed out none too kindly.

Stung by the attorney's dismissive attitude, Kit could only stare at him in silence.

"Your comments to Mr. Gilmore yesterday, as related to me by him, also seem to indicate that you believe Nathan wouldn't be hurt by being kept from his father. Isn't that true, Ms. Davenport? Or am I mistaken—"

"John," Simon said, quietly interrupting in a tone that had about it an air of command. "Kit acted on misinformation she got from Nathan's mother, as I've already explained to you. She knows now that I didn't abandon Lucy Kane or my son intentionally—at least I believe she knows that now."

Kit nodded, grateful to him for defending her, as Simon met her gaze with a questioning look. But almost immediately she wondered if maybe Simon and his attorney were playing good cop, bad cop with her to throw her off balance. An appreciative woman would certainly be much more amenable to his dictates. And he'd just shown her that he cared enough about her to stand up to his own attorney on her behalf.

Suddenly unsure what to think, much less what to say, she looked at Isaac pleadingly, willing him to step into the fray.

"So, we are in agreement that the DNA testing will be conducted as soon as possible," he said, returning her gaze with a reassuring smile.

"Yes, of course, just as soon as possible," she replied.

"I'd like to stipulate that we all understand *as soon as possible* to be within the next seven days," John Mahoney said, raising Kit's hackles all over again.

"I'd like to suggest that Kit and Nathan drive down to Missoula with me so she won't have to make the three-hour trip on her own with him," Simon interjected before she could snap at his attorney. To her, he added, "Whenever you'd like to go, since you'll have to arrange to be away from the diner all day, too."

Again Kit felt a wave of gratitude toward Simon, and again suspicion followed, but only momentarily. No matter how self-serving his reasons for suggesting that they drive down to Missoula together, it would be to her advantage, as well.

Traffic on the two-lane road, especially heading home, would be heavy even this early in the tourist season. And she didn't like the idea of having to drive her aging car so far alone, either. Getting stuck on the road, having to wait for a tow truck with a fussy child, would be as scary as it would be miserable.

"How about Friday?" she suggested, to show just how cooperative she was willing to be. "Bonnie is scheduled to work all day, and Sara, Nathan's sitter, can help out, too, since I won't be needing her to watch him."

"Friday it is, then," Simon replied with a smile he, too, must have meant to be reassuring.

It was, in fact, but only until John Mahoney spoke again.

"Now let's address the matter of visitation," he said, sounding much too pleased with himself for Kit's peace of mind.

"Visitation?" she repeated in a high, tight tone of voice.

She had to admit that Mahoney was good even as she looked at Isaac again, seeking his help. Once more he attempted a supportive smile, but Kit now understood all too well that there were limits to what he could do for her if hostilities were to be avoided.

"I believe it would be good for both my client and for the child if Mr. Gilmore is allowed to start spending some time with Nathan so they can begin to get to know each other. I'm suggesting the visitation be supervised initially by Ms. Davenport so as not to upset the child unnecessarily. I realize that he's suffered one major loss already. I also realize he's begun to bond with Ms. Davenport in a…pseudoparental relationship. But by gradually allowing Nathan to feel comfortable with Mr. Gilmore, I believe we can avoid any undo trauma once the custody issue has been settled."

In other words, once Simon is given full custody of Nathan, Kit thought to herself, the stab of pain that shot through her heart making her want to curl up in a little ball.

Then *she* would be the one doing the visiting, but only if Simon was amenable.

"I agree with John," Isaac said, not surprisingly.

He, too, had to see how the custody issue would eventually be decided, and he had already warned her about the primacy of parental rights.

"I also suggest that we allow Ms. Davenport and Mr. Gilmore to work out dates and times, again to avoid any delay that would occur if we were to wait for a court order," Isaac added. "Is that all right with you, Kit, and you, Mr. Gilmore?"

Together Simon and she answered yes without exchanging so much as a glance.

"Very good—very good, indeed." Isaac beamed like a proud parent, pleased with his children's good behavior. "Now, Mr. Gilmore, I'll give you the information on the lab in Missoula so you can set up an appointment for Friday. Perhaps the two of you can decided on a schedule for visitation when you're together then. Anything further that we need to discuss today, John?"

"Not that I can think of." Mr. Mahoney stood and held out his hand to Isaac. "Good to see you again."

"And you, John," Isaac replied as he, too, stood to shake the other man's hand.

"How are you enjoying semiretirement here in Belle?" Mr. Mahoney asked.

"Quite a lot actually, although I'm also glad to have a little work come my way occasionally."

Kit stared at the two attorneys as they bantered back and forth, more like friends than adversaries now that certain issues had been resolved to their mutual satisfaction.

She felt slightly betrayed as she stood, as well, her

purse clutched in her hands, and stepped out of the way so John Mahoney and Simon Gilmore could make their way to the door. She intended to say as much once she and Isaac were alone, but he gestured for her to proceed him out of his office along with the others.

"Why don't you and Mr. Gilmore take a moment to firm up your plans for Friday?" he suggested. "We can talk again next week. Then you can let me know how Nathan's adjusting to the visitation, all right?"

"All right," she replied.

It wasn't really, but Isaac seemed more interested in discussing his latest fly-fishing adventure with Simon's attorney than in listening to her vent her frustration over how their meeting had concluded. And Simon had hung back, waiting for her so they could talk as Isaac had said they should.

"Are you sure Friday will be all right?" he asked as they paused on the sidewalk outside Isaac's office.

John Mahoney had walked on to his car after a last word to Simon that he'd be in touch, leaving them alone at last.

"As all right as any other day would be," she replied in a grudging tone, making a point of looking away.

She couldn't help but wonder if she'd allowed herself to be bulldozed into doing something that she'd ultimately regret. She could drive to Missoula on her own. She'd done it often enough in the past. But it was not only unnecessary, it would also be stressful and exhausting. What purpose would it serve except to salve her pride?

"I understand how you feel, Kit. Really, I do," Simon said, putting a hand on her shoulder to gain her attention. "Is it so hard for you to understand how *I* feel? You've had

Nathan in your life since he was born. Maybe not on a daily basis because you've been away at college, but at least you've been able to watch him grow and change the past two years. I want to get to know my son, Kit, and I need your help to do it. Don't be angry with me. Just…understand, if you can."

He had asked the same thing of her earlier. *Please…understand…* She had wanted to then and she wanted to now. But with understanding had to come acceptance that within a few weeks, maybe a few months at most, she would lose the only person left in her life that she loved.

"I'm trying," she said, shrugging off Simon's hand, the warmth of his touch too unsettling to allow her to think straight. "But I'm afraid it's going to take me a while to come to terms with the fact that you have every intention of taking Nathan away from me, regardless of what I say or do."

"I'm not planning to disappear off the face of the earth with him," Simon countered quietly.

"Maybe not just yet, but eventually…" She looked down the quiet street for a long moment, blinking back yet another unwanted prickle of tears in her eyes.

"I don't think either one of us can predict what will happen in our lives eventually."

"Certainly not me," she agreed, businesslike once again as she met his gaze. She would have never thought Simon would come back to Belle and claim that he had a right to Lucy's child. "You'll make the appointment at the lab for Friday?"

"I thought we could aim for eleven or eleven-thirty. That means we'll have to leave Belle by eight o'clock, eight-thirty at the latest."

"You'd better aim to be at the diner by seven-thirty," she advised. "We'll have to transfer Nathan's car seat to your SUV and that might take some time. We'll also have to make at least one rest stop along the way so he can stretch his legs. Otherwise he'll get really fussy."

"Okay, I'll be at the diner at seven-thirty Friday morning."

"Let me know if there are any changes timewise, so I can make arrangements accordingly."

"I'll do that."

"Well, until Friday…"

Kit's voice drifted off as she looked up at Simon—really allowed herself to look at him. In his eyes, she saw something akin to longing, but for what, she didn't know. She realized, however, that if he held out his arms to her, if he offered her just that small amount of physical contact, she would accept it without a second thought.

Here was the guy who had been almost like a brother to her during the years they'd grown up together. She wouldn't have thought twice about asking him to help her now if only *he* weren't the problem. But he was the problem, and that meant she was all on her own now.

Chapter Six

It had taken every ounce of willpower Simon possessed to stay away from the Dinner Belle Diner on Thursday. He hadn't thought Kit would turn him away if he asked to see Nathan. Not after the session they'd had with their attorneys. She might have felt pressured, though, and resentful as a result.

He wanted her help, *needed* her help, getting to know his son, as he'd told her once already. But he didn't want that help to be grudgingly given. He wanted Kit to think of the two of them as a team working together for everyone's benefit, hers included.

Unfortunately, Simon wasn't sure how to convince her of that, though. She seemed so determined to hold herself aloof, and to deny, as well, the possibility that they could rekindle the fond feelings they'd once had for each other.

Lucy had brought them together as friends in the past. He wanted to believe that Nathan could do the same now.

But first he had to earn Kit's trust—no easy task, he had to admit, even if she had begun to doubt the truthfulness of Lucy's tale.

To get his mind off the upheaval in his life, Simon helped his mother fix up one of the spare bedrooms for his son. He had hauled his own baby bed down from the attic along with other assorted items dating back to his childhood that Deanna insisted would come in handy.

Simon hadn't gotten an especially warm welcome from his parents when he'd arrived at the ranch Tuesday morning, but then he hadn't expected one. Based on the glimpse of Nathan that his father had apparently gotten when he had seen Kit with the little boy at the hardware store, both he and Simon's mother had assumed the worst. Simon had been able to convince them of the truth—he'd never knowingly abandon Lucy or his baby—though not as easily as he'd hoped.

Finally believing that he hadn't known Nathan was his son until his return to Belle, however, his parents had been the ones to suggest that he hire John Mahoney as his legal counsel. They had also begun to look forward to formally meeting their only grandchild just as soon as Simon had a chance to arrange it with Kit.

Pulling up in front of the Dinner Belle Diner at exactly seven-thirty Friday morning, Simon hoped Kit would be agreeable to that particular suggestion. He also acknowledged that finding Kit in a tractable mood was likely to be a long shot, and he'd be wise not to count on having such luck on their first outing together, forced upon her as it was.

As Simon switched off the SUV's engine, a jolt of anticipation squeezed his gut. He was excited about seeing his son, of course. But in all honesty, he knew that it was seeing Kit again that had him all hot and bothered.

She was such a scrappy little thing, no pushover at all, and she'd always had high standards. Though he couldn't say exactly why it mattered to him, Simon wanted to measure up in her eyes. He knew that he wasn't going to need her acceptance or her approval to gain custody of his son. John Mahoney had assured him of that. But he would feel like a better person with her support than he would without it.

Determined to stand his ground no matter what kind of attitude Kit threw his way, Simon took his key from the SUV's ignition. Before he could exit the vehicle, however, the diner's front door opened and Kit stepped onto the sidewalk. Looking slim and sexy in a narrow denim skirt and a sleeveless red T-shirt that barely covered her midriff, she held what appeared to be a child's car seat. Without the slightest hesitation, she walked up to the SUV, opened the back passenger door and heaved the contraption into place, centering it on the bench-style seat.

"Can you strap this thing down while I get the diaper bag and stroller? I've packed a cooler with juice and soft drinks and a bottle for Nathan, too. Also, a thermos of coffee—I'm still about a quart low. Have you eaten breakfast yet or should I wrap up one of George's egg-bacon-and-biscuit sandwiches for you? I'm having one myself once we're on the road."

She spoke quickly, her tone brisk and businesslike, though Simon also detected an underlying hint of uneasiness in her voice. She didn't look at him, either—not once the whole time she rattled on, listing quite impressively how competently she'd covered all the bases, preparing for their drive to Missoula in ways he wouldn't have considered necessary without her prompting.

As he joined her on the sidewalk, she turned back to the diner. Simon thought about letting her go, but couldn't do it. He knew she was trying to put up a wall between them—though ever so politely—and he wasn't having any of that. Not when they were about to spend an entire day together.

"Hey," he said softly, catching her by the arm in a firm yet gentle grip. "Good morning to you, too, Kit Davenport."

She had the good grace to blush as she met his gaze. Then her glance skittered away.

"Sorry, I have a lot on my mind," she said in a surprisingly apologetic tone. Looking up at him again as he kept a hold on her arm, she offered him a very tiny, very wry smile. "But that's no reason to be rude to you, is it?"

"I wouldn't say you were rude, just a little distracted." Relieved that she seemed as willing as he to at least try to be on friendly terms that day, Simon smiled, too. He gave her arm an encouraging squeeze before letting her go, then asked, "Anything else I can do to give you a hand besides securing Nathan's car seat?"

"Unless you're an engineering genius, the car seat should keep you occupied for a minimum of fifteen minutes. I'll have everything else loaded and ready to go by then," she replied, her smile becoming just the slightest bit cocky. "Do you want a biscuit sandwich or not?"

"Yes, please. I'd like to have one as long as it's not going to cause you any extra work."

"None at all. I wasn't very hungry myself earlier this morning. I thought maybe you wouldn't have been, either, so I asked George to have some ready to go just in case."

"You're right. I wasn't hungry earlier, either, but I am now."

"You haven't even begun to work up a real appetite yet, struggling with the car seat. Maybe I should add some of George's locally famous cinnamon rolls to our breakfast bag, as well."

"Oh, yeah, for sure, although I can't imagine how securing a car seat could be as difficult as you're making it sound. I managed to figure out the bottle warmer, didn't I?"

"Car seats are a little trickier—something you've obviously never had the opportunity to find out...until now," she advised him, the grin she flashed before going into the diner again bordering on truly wicked.

As good as her word, Kit had everything loaded into the SUV long before Simon had even begun to figure out how to attach the seat belt to the car seat to hold it firmly in place.

"Told you so," she said, sounding pleased with herself as she stood on the sidewalk, holding Nathan in her arms.

"Yes, you certainly did," he agreed ruefully. "Why don't you let me hold Nathan while you give me a much-needed and greatly appreciated lesson in Baby Paraphernalia 101?"

Kit hesitated for a moment, eyeing him thoughtfully, all trace of her earlier good humor gone. Her grip on Nathan, who also gazed at him thoughtfully, seemed to tighten incrementally. But then she drew a breath and appeared to give herself a mental shake.

"Want to go to Si—um, your daddy, for a minute, little buddy?" she asked the child with a tip of her head in Simon's direction.

Simon eyed Kit with surprise as well as gratitude. Hearing her refer to him to his son in such a manner warmed him. She might be reluctant, but she now seemed willing at last to accept his presence in her life, and Nathan's, and make the inevitable transition as smooth as possible. Nathan, too, appeared to be agreeable.

"Dahee?" he repeated, pointing one small finger at Simon.

"Yes, your daddy," Kit answered as she shifted the child in her arms, then held him out to Simon.

For one long moment, Simon hesitated, suddenly nervous. He wasn't used to handling small children, and he'd only held Nathan one time. But then, love and longing for the son he had only just found eased the knot in his belly. He took the grinning, bright-eyed little boy from Kit and settled him comfortably against his shoulder. This precious child was *his son,* he thought, his heart swelling with justifiable pride.

In a matter of minutes, Kit had the car seat secured. Simon missed at least half of her instructions, so intent was he on assessing every aspect of his son's youthful features. Dark curls soft as down; equally dark eyelashes, long and lush, fanning onto pale, porcelain skin whenever he blinked his sparkling blue eyes; sturdy body dressed in tiny jeans and a bright yellow T-shirt; feet clad in yellow socks and little sneakers.

"Yellow socks?" he questioned as Kit stepped back and waved a see-how-easy-it-was hand at the car seat. "My son is wearing yellow socks?"

"They match his T-shirt," Kit pointed out. "They look so cute, too, don't they, little buddy?"

Reaching out, she tweaked Nathan on the foot, and he giggled joyfully in reply.

"I agree that they match his shirt," Simon allowed, adopting a manly tone.

He put Nathan in his car seat then looked to Kit again after fumbling with the straps meant to hold the child safely in place.

"But you don't think they're cute?" Kit prodded, her tone teasing as she stepped forward to buckle Nathan into his seat with a snap here and a click there.

Prudently, Simon didn't respond to Kit's comment. Instead he said to Nathan, "Have to get you some boots, young man. A guy wearing yellow socks could get a lot of razzing around this town."

"Hey, little boots would be adorable, too," Kit said.

"Yeah, but in a *guy* kind of way, right buddy?"

Nathan kicked his legs and chattered nonsense in reply.

"And guys will be guys, won't they?" Kit asked.

She shot Simon a look not altogether approving.

"It's what we do best," he replied, offering her his most charming grin.

Not the least bit impressed, Kit fished Nathan's teddy bear from the diaper bag, tucked it beside the little boy and closed the passenger door.

"We'd better get going," she advised. "Otherwise we'll be late for our appointment."

Not waiting for him to respond, she climbed into the front passenger seat and fastened her seat belt, her expression suddenly much more serious than it had been just a few moments earlier.

Frowning, too, Simon got behind the steering wheel and started the engine. Glancing over at Kit, he saw that she was sitting with her hands tightly clasped in her lap, a stony look on her face.

They had begun the day so well—in fact, much better than Simon had expected, all things considered. Their bantering back and forth had seemed to be as enjoyable to Kit as it had been to him. Yet in the space of just a minute or two she had withdrawn from him as completely as she could while still sitting next to him in his SUV.

"Was it something I said?" he asked, speaking his thoughts aloud as he steered the vehicle away from the curb.

She cast him a quizzical glance as if uncertain why he'd posed such a question. But the tinge of red tinting the fair skin of her face assured him that she understood quite well the reason for it.

"Because I really do like Nathan's little yellow socks," he added, wanting more than anything to tease her out of whatever discomfort she seemed to be feeling.

"He'll be able to get away with them for another year or two before he becomes bully-bait. Buying him some boots is definitely a good idea, though," Kit said.

Opening the brown paper bag she'd stowed on the floor by her feet, she took out two cups of coffee and the biscuit sandwiches she'd packed for their trip.

"Coffee black, right?" she asked.

"Right," he replied as she set the cups in the cup holders on the either side of the console.

"Biscuit?"

"Yes, please."

She unwrapped one of the sandwiches for him, releasing the mouth-watering aroma of biscuit and bacon, and passed it to him along with a paper napkin. She unwrapped another for herself, as well, then broke off a piece of biscuit for Nathan. The little boy took it from her eagerly and munched on it with obvious delight.

"So he's mostly eating regular people food?" Simon asked, glancing at Nathan's reflection in the rearview mirror.

"Oh, yes, he'll eat just about anything now. You just have to make sure to keep the bits and pieces small enough for him to manage. It's not a good idea to leave him completely alone with his food, though, in case he starts to choke. But I haven't had that happen yet. Of course, I have a tendency to hover, so if he puts too much in his mouth at one time I have him spit some of it out right away, which he really likes to do."

"I'm thinking I have an awful lot to learn about caring for a two-year-old," Simon admitted.

In fact, hearing Kit talk so easily and so knowledgeably about the intricacies of the supposedly simple task of feeding the little boy a meal left him feeling slightly overwhelmed. That was only one small responsibility he'd be taking on full-time in the very near future.

"There is a lot to keep in mind, especially now that Nathan's started walking. He's very bright and thus also very inquisitive. Babyproofing the apartment has been a real challenge. Every time I think there couldn't possibly be anything else lying around for him to stick in his mouth, he finds a button under the bed or I forget and leave a pen on the coffee table."

"You seem to have everything under control. You also know a lot more about child minding than I do," he acknowledged.

"I learned a lot from Lucy. She was so good with Nathan. She loved him so much from the very start."

Wadding up the empty wrapper that had held her biscuit sandwich, Kit spared Simon a reproachful look, then turned away to stare out the side window, her expression mournful once again.

"I would have loved Nathan from the very start, too, if

Lucy had given me the chance," Simon countered, unable to keep the defensiveness he felt from his tone.

Kit responded evenly, "If Lucy didn't want you to know that you were the father of her child then she must have had a good reason."

"Meaning what, exactly?" Simon demanded. The merest hint of anger was now evident in his voice. "That I have some hidden tendency toward monstrous behavior, and thus have to be kept from my own child? You have to know that isn't true, Kit. Lucy had to make me look like the bad guy. Otherwise she wouldn't have been the injured party, and that was the one way she could guarantee she'd gain your sympathy. Her own mother wouldn't have lifted a finger to help her—helping Lucy would have interfered too much with her drinking—but Lucy knew you and your mother would under the right circumstances."

"You make her sound like a scheming witch." Kit's voice, too, had an angry edge to it now.

"There's a hell of a lot more chance of Lucy being a scheming witch than of me either abandoning my child in the past or being a danger to him now. If I didn't want anything to do with having a child, why would I be willing to take custody of a toddler three years later? And if I'm such a fearsome beast, why am I docilely driving you to Missoula when I could bop you over the head, dump you down a canyon and do God only knows what awful things to that precious little boy sitting quietly in his car seat?"

Obviously caught off guard, Kit turned slowly in her seat to face him, stunned by the vehemence of his response. Though Simon kept his eyes on the road winding away ahead of them, he couldn't ignore completely the intensity of her gaze on him. He wondered what was going through her mind, then thought he was probably better off not knowing.

They had seemed to find some common ground earlier—a place where they could be not exactly friends, but not enemies, either. Then Kit had brought Lucy into the mix and he'd lost every gain he'd made with her.

"I don't think you're a monster or a fearsome beast," she said contritely, her soft voice finally cutting through the heavy silence surrounding them. "But I don't like thinking that Lucy could have been as devious as you've made her out to be without a very good reason."

"I don't like thinking that of her, either, Kit," Simon admitted. "Hell, I truly believed I was in love with her three years ago. Then she told me she was having someone else's baby and nearly broke my heart. I got over the hurt a long time ago, but finding out about Nathan…" He paused meaningfully, then added, "Let's just say it's been a reminder that Lucy would sometimes have a rather casual regard for the truth. I'd think you would feel the same way, too."

"It's hard for me not to give her the benefit of the doubt, but then she never hurt me as badly as she apparently hurt you. She did entrust me with her son's safekeeping, though. I can't just turn my back on that responsibility because you're now claiming that you have a right to him. I can't, and I *won't*, dismiss the *why* of Lucy's behavior out of hand. She obviously had reservations about you, and as Nathan's guardian, I feel it's my duty to keep that in mind. I'm not going to stand by quietly and let you take Nathan away from me, either—not without proof that you can— and will—take good care of him."

"So I'm guilty until proven innocent on Lucy's say-so alone?" Simon asked with a growing sense of futility.

How could he defend himself against the mental gyrations of a dead woman who had considered lying a viable and beneficial life skill?

"It's not so much about you being guilty as me being cautious for Nathan's sake. You would expect that of anyone looking after him, wouldn't you?" Kit insisted, maneuvering him neatly into a corner.

Admitting that only a fool would attempt to argue that particular point, Simon responded with a curt "Yes, of course."

"Would you like more coffee from the thermos?" she asked, once again cordial.

Another curt affirmation got him a refill. Kit also added coffee to her cup before recapping the thermos. She glanced back at Nathan, who, Simon saw in the rearview mirror, was dozing in his car seat, his teddy bear clutched in one hand. Then she took a paperback novel from her purse, opened the book to the page she'd marked with a card and began to read, a serenely and supremely satisfied smile on her pretty face.

Not only had she gotten in the last word, she had also ended their conversation standing on high moral ground. Forced to admit that he, too, would be cautious on Nathan's behalf, he could no longer fault her for questioning either his character or his intentions. In fact, he had put himself in the position of having to prove to her that he was worthy of taking custody of his own son.

Frustrated, Simon wanted to point out the unfairness of Kit's attitude. But the more he'd argued with her, the darker his mood had become, spoiling what had started out as a nice day in supposedly good company. He would have been better off letting her sit beside him in silence from the start of their trip.

They each had the same ultimate goal—Nathan's well-being. Attaining that goal was all that mattered to Simon. Kit could attempt to shut him out in the process, but that wouldn't change the outcome. He was Nathan Kane's father. Barring any unforeseen difficulties, he would have custody of his son by summer's end, whether Kit approved of him or not. He didn't need her on his side. Now if only he could convince himself that he didn't *want* her on his side, either, all would be right with his world.

Chapter Seven

Initially, Kit was pleased with the way that she'd ended her conversation with Simon. He couldn't condemn her for refusing to take him at his word. Her suspicion of him came from her love for Nathan, and her desire to keep the little boy safe as Simon would want anyone in charge of his son to do.

But Simon had awakened certain memories in Kit's mind—memories of Lucy's behavior toward her in the past, behavior that had often been thoughtless and self-serving. Like Simon, Kit had ignored her friend's less appealing tendencies. So many times she'd told herself that Lucy didn't mean any harm even when she would have had to know she was acting in a hurtful way.

As they traveled down the highway in silence, Kit pretended to read, but her attention wasn't really on the printed pages she turned at regular intervals. Instead she wondered what Lucy had hoped to gain by ending her relationship with Simon.

Until Lucy had told her of his willful abandonment, Kit had always thought he was the kindest, most decent man among the many who had been attracted to her friend. She couldn't know how he'd treated Lucy when they were alone, but Lucy had never once acted as if she had reason to be anything but head-over-heels in love with him.

Or maybe, Kit amended, what passed for love in Lucy's repertoire of emotions.

Abandoned as a child by her father, and left to her own devices by an alcoholic mother, Lucy had learned early on to use her looks and charm to her advantage, playing on the sympathy of anyone who gave her half a chance. With shy, quiet Kit, whose own father had died when she was only six years old, and her generous mother, she had soon found a haven where there was always a hearty meal and warm bed waiting for her, even after Kit had gone away to college.

But Simon would have been able to provide an equally good life for Lucy. He had a college education, he was about to start a wonderful job in Seattle and he had wanted to marry her. He had told Kit as much on more than one occasion.

Had she been the one Simon Gilmore loved three years ago, Kit thought now, she would have accepted his proposal in a heartbeat. Immediately, a hot flush suffused her face. She glanced at Simon surreptitiously, wondering what had prompted that previously unacknowledged conviction to pop into her head at that particular moment.

Simon had always been part of Lucy's domain, and Kit had always considered him off-limits. To do otherwise would have meant the end of their friendship, and insecure, stable Kit had always believed that she needed outgoing, gregarious Lucy's friendship as much as Lucy needed hers.

Though looking back, Kit thought that might not have really been true. She had done fine on her own away at college. She had become an independent, self-sufficient young adult. Lucy, on the other hand, hadn't made any real changes in the life she'd lived, even after Nathan was born.

Kit could understand why Lucy had told her and her mother that Simon had abandoned her—for the exact reason he had presented. Dolores had been so sympathetic with her plight that she'd insisted on Lucy moving into the apartment with her immediately, and Lucy had stayed there until the day she died. She had helped out at the diner, but with free room and board and a baby-sitter on hand, she hadn't been forced to put in long hours. She had also been able to party as often as she wanted.

Yes, Lucy had loved Nathan and she had cared for him. But she hadn't had any qualms about leaving him with Dolores, and then with Kit, for several days at a time. Nor had she been inclined to work harder at the diner when Dolores had become ill. Instead, she had called Kit to let her know she was needed back in Belle.

Kit had loved Lucy like a sister, and she hated feeling disloyal to her now. But suddenly she couldn't help wondering if she'd been giving the wrong person the benefit of the doubt.

Glancing at Simon again, she thought about saying as much to him. She was the one responsible for the icy silence hanging over them, and she should be the one to break it. But the frowning twist of his lips and the rigid line of his jaw offered her no encouragement.

"More coffee?" she asked again, turning to face him at last.

"No thanks," he replied, his gaze firmly fixed on the road.

"There's a rest area up ahead along the lake," she ventured a few minutes later after noting that Nathan had awakened from his nap. "Maybe we should stop and let the little guy stretch his legs."

"Fine with me."

Fifteen minutes later, they were back in the SUV again after a diaper change for Nathan, trips to the rest room for her and Simon and a short walk along the shore of Flat Head Lake. Kit ventured quietly, "You know, Simon, I've been thinking—"

"Mind if I turn on the radio?" he asked, cutting her off in a matter-of-fact tone.

"No, of course not," she replied.

"Sure it won't bother you while you're reading?"

She had purposely left her book in her purse as Simon had pulled out of the rest area parking lot. But she could certainly take a hint.

"Not at all."

With a quiet sigh Kit dug out her book as Simon tuned into a station playing popular music from the eighties. She'd done such a good job of shutting down their earlier line of communication that it seemed she was going to have to live with it—at least for the time being. She'd find a way to get Simon to talk to her again, though. He wasn't the type to stay angry for long.

He also needed her help with Nathan. She'd let him off the hook, changing the little boy's stinky diaper at the rest area, but she fully intended to let him tackle the stroller on his own once they reached Missoula. Considering his history with the car seat, he'd be warming up to her again real soon.

Smiling to herself, she opened her book, then sensed Simon's gaze on her.

"What?" he asked, sounding suspicious.

"Oh, nothing…."

She glanced at him, shot him a wicked grin and looked down at her book again, finally able to focus on the story unfolding upon its pages.

They arrived in Missoula with time to spare and quickly found the lab, located near the university campus. To Kit's amazement, and disappointment, Simon not only set up Nathan's stroller, but also secured the little boy in it with swift and silent efficiency. The few comments he made were directed at Nathan, as well. Kit could have been a total stranger standing on the sidewalk for all the attention he paid her. Once again, she admitted that she had only herself to blame.

You couldn't expect a man to defend himself against your distrust, let him know he was fighting a losing battle, then think he'd allow you to engage him in any way again, Kit reminded herself.

She followed after Simon as he pushed the stroller the short distance to the front entrance of the lab, then hurried ahead to open the door. She tried to catch his eye with an ingratiating smile and received only an icy, albeit polite, thank-you in return.

The staff members at the lab were extremely professional. After Simon checked in with the receptionist, they waited only a few minutes before a technician took them to separate rooms—Simon in one, Kit and Nathan in another.

Up until that moment, Nathan had been happily studying his new surroundings while flirting shamelessly with any female who caught his eye. But when Simon disappeared behind a closed door and he was left alone with Kit, the little boy's lower lip began to tremble.

"Dahee…Dahee…Dahee," he cried, kicking his feet and waving his teddy bear while also trying to wriggle out of his stroller.

"It's okay, baby," Kit soothed. She released the straps that held him in place, then stood him up beside her. "Daddy will be back soon."

Obviously unwilling to wait, Nathan toddled toward the door, still calling "Dahee…Dahee…Dahee—" He stopped suddenly, though, when the door handle turned and the tech entered again, carrying a metal tray filled with all sorts of interesting items.

"Well, hello again, young man," the tech said.

Temporarily diverted, Nathan stared in awe at the tall, slim woman with long red hair, then bestowed on her his most engaging grin.

"Men!" She glanced at Kit with a wry smile. "They're all the same, aren't they, no matter the age?"

"Seems so, doesn't it?" Kit smiled, too, as Nathan ran back to her, then shot a coy look over his shoulder at the tech.

"This will only take a few minutes. I just need to take some swabs of the inside of his mouth," the tech explained, setting her tray on the counter. "Think he'll sit on your lap?"

"For a few minutes," Kit replied. She led Nathan to a chair and lifted him onto her lap, then asked, "Do you want to show the pretty lady how many bright and shiny teeth you have?"

Nathan gladly obliged and, good as her word, the tech took the necessary swabs before he could even begin to think about fussing. Kit then tried to put him back in the stroller, but he wasn't having any of that. Instead, he chose to help her push it down the hallway to the reception room. There, to his delight, and Kit's relief, Simon joined them almost immediately.

Apparently as charmed as his son by the attractive lab tech, Simon lingered in the doorway, exchanging a last word with her about when to expect the test results. Then he scooped Nathan into his arms, gave the chortling child a hug and settled him into the stroller without any complaint.

Kit watched them with a sudden sense of alienation. For the first time since Simon had come back to town, she realized that her presence there wasn't really needed—*she* wasn't really needed. Simon and his son appeared to be perfectly capable of getting along without her.

Turning away from them, she walked to the door, her feelings unaccountably hurt. She should be glad for Nathan's sake that he had taken so well to Simon, and that Simon had taken so well to him. Nathan would prosper greatly with his father's love. And the fact that Nathan now had a father to love him didn't mean he would no longer love *her*.

But he was so young and his attachment to her so new. How long would he remember her once Simon took him away? She could ask for visitation, as Isaac had suggested, but that might only confuse the child, especially if Simon had a special woman in his life—

Kit barely had time to deal with *that* as-yet-unacknowledged possibility when Nathan let out a shriek of undisguised distress. Halfway out the door, she turned to see the little boy reaching out to her from the stroller, his teddy bear forgotten on the floor.

"Hey, wait for us," Simon said, collecting the bear as he rolled the stroller toward her. The look he gave her was both reproachful and appealing. "Otherwise the little guy's going to be mighty unhappy."

"And the big guy?" Kit asked with an apologetic smile.

"He'd rather not be left alone just yet with a mighty unhappy little guy," Simon admitted, flashing a rueful grin.

"It's going to happen eventually," she said—a reminder to herself as well as him.

"I know, but I'd rather have you teach me some parenting skills first."

Again, Nathan shrieked as they stopped on the sidewalk by the SUV.

"What now?" Simon asked, looking first at the little boy, then looking at Kit in obvious confusion.

"Parenting skill number one," Kit said, taking the bear from Simon and handing it to Nathan. "Always make sure the boy has his bear. If shrieking continues, check diaper while also trying to recall last time boy was fed."

Nathan shrieked again, waving the bear at them.

"Diaper?" Simon asked.

"Probably, but I imagine he's hungry, too."

"So we'd better change his diaper, then find a place to eat, right?"

"Right."

"We could drive downtown and find a restaurant," Simon suggested.

"We could also head over to the fast-food place out by the highway that also has an indoor play area," Kit said.

"Should we be feeding him burgers and fries?" Simon appeared genuinely concerned.

"Only on the occasions when we also want to tire him out enough in the accompanying play area so that he'll nap instead of shriek most of the way back to Belle."

"Point well taken," Simon acknowledged with another rueful grin. "So I guess you'd better change his diaper, huh?"

"Actually I was thinking you could change his diaper this time."

"But I've never changed a diaper."

"Oh, it's much easier than securing the car seat, and I'll be more than happy to give you instructions," Kit said, smiling up at him as she released Nathan from the stroller.

"Gee, thanks," Simon muttered, then rolled his eyes as he took the little boy from her. "Oh, man, am I smelling what I think I'm smelling?"

"Oh, yes…you most certainly are."

Kit concluded that there were few things as funny, or as endearing, as watching a grown man's first attempt at changing a busy two-year-old child's stinky diaper. Simon did a fairly good job.

There was a moment when his face paled noticeably and he shot an entreating gaze her way. But when she made no move to come to his rescue, he soldiered on with grim determination. Of course, she gave him no alternative. Still, he didn't grouse about it or whine as a lesser man might have.

Simon seemed to enjoy the fast-food restaurant as much as Nathan did—not the meal they ate, so much as the play area where he followed behind his son protectively, helping him up the ladder of the little slide, spinning him slowly on a miniature merry-go-round and watching him jump into the pool of plastic balls over and over again.

He didn't seem to mind staying until Nathan's eyes began to droop, either—definitely a good thing. Nathan was ready for his bottle and a nap once he was secured in his car seat, guaranteeing them, as Kit had predicted, a relatively peaceful drive back to Belle.

She offered to take a turn at the wheel, but Simon said he didn't mind driving. Grateful for the chance to rest, Kit didn't argue. Neither did she mind that Simon played the radio. She felt comfortable now, sitting quietly beside him, and she wanted to savor the moment, knowing in her heart how fleeting it would be.

She had thought about the future—a future without Nathan—enough for one day. And she didn't have the emotional energy to delve into, not to mention argue about, the past with Simon any more than she already had. For just a little while, silence really did seem like a golden choice to her, and luckily Simon apparently agreed.

Kit wasn't sure when she fell asleep—probably not long after Simon pulled onto the highway. When she awoke again she was surprised not only by how refreshed she felt, but also how close to Belle they were.

She couldn't remember the last time she'd slept so soundly for such a relatively long stretch of time. Being the one solely responsible for Nathan had her always on high alert. But with Simon sharing the obligation that afternoon, she had finally been able to relax her vigil just a little.

"Hey, sleepyhead," he said softly, glancing at her, his smile indulgent.

"Hey, yourself."

She shifted and stretched in her seat, then looked over her shoulder to check on Nathan. Miraculously, he was still asleep.

"You must have been tired," Simon observed.

"Must have been," she agreed in a languid tone.

"Feel better now?"

"Lots better. You must be tired, though. Belle to Missoula and back again in one day is a lot of driving for one person to do. You should have woken me up. Then you could have had a break, too. I *am* a careful driver, you know."

"You looked so peaceful I didn't have the heart to disturb you. I appreciate the offer, though. Next road trip we take together, I promise I'll let you help with the driving. How's that?"

"Fine with me," Kit said, though she wondered when he thought they'd take another trip together.

They hadn't actually gone to Missoula for the fun of it. In fact, their relationship was such that she couldn't imagine them doing anything together for the fun of it. Although being with Simon hadn't been a hardship.

Simon's thoughts seemed to follow a similar track. He didn't say anything more for several minutes. Finally, she looked over at him surreptitiously and saw that a frown furrowed his forehead. He appeared to have something serious on his mind, and she was afraid that whatever it happened to be, she wasn't going to like it.

They were on the outskirts of town when Simon spoke again. Kit had been gazing out the side window, steeling herself for something troublesome, but still, the sound of his voice startled her.

"I was wondering…" he began in a tone that was not only questioning but also very determined.

"What?" Kit asked, shifting in her seat so that she faced him, her own voice guarded.

"I'd like to take Nathan out to the ranch so my parents can meet him," he said.

Kit stared at Simon in shocked silence, every fiber of her being wanting to shout *no, no, no*, though she knew he had every right to make such a request of her.

As if aware of her unspoken response, Simon kept his gaze on the road ahead as he continued.

"I thought Sunday afternoon would be good. The diner's closed then, so you could go with us…if you wanted to."

Relief washed over Kit in a wave. He hadn't intended to take Nathan from her, after all—at least not yet. He had simply wanted his parents to have an opportunity to see their grandson, up close and personal, and he'd offered to include her in the outing even though he didn't have to.

"Yes, Sunday afternoon would be good," she agreed, looking out the side window again.

"How would it be if I picked you up about two o'clock? That will give Nathan time to have a nap, won't it?"

"Two o'clock will be just fine."

"And you'll come with us?"

"You won't mind?"

"Of course not," Simon replied. His voice softening, he put a hand over the fist she'd clenched against her thigh and squeezed gently, reassuringly. "They're nice people, my folks. They think a lot of you and how well you've cared for Nathan. They would have helped you…. Hell, they would have helped Lucy if they'd known…."

"I realize that…now," Kit said, opening her fist so that she could hold on to Simon's hand.

He was being incredibly kind, not shutting her out completely from the Gilmore family unit, and she was such a sucker for kindness. Had there not been a console between them, she might have even been tempted to rest her head on his shoulder.

"I'm glad."

Again Simon squeezed her hand to emphasize his words, and Kit couldn't help but glance at him with a sudden pang of longing. How could Lucy have run this man out of her life?

Simon turned, too, his gaze searching. He started to speak, but before he could say more than her name, Nathan awakened with a cranky cry, cutting him off.

"Diaper change, right?" Simon said as he put his hand back on the steering wheel and guided the SUV to the curb in front of the diner, now closed for the day.

"Right," Kit replied. Mentally shrugging off her disappointment at Nathan's untimely interruption, she eyed Simon with a teasing smile. "Want to come upstairs and do the honors?"

"Would it be completely callous of me to offer to unload the SUV and carry everything up to the apartment instead?"

"Not *completely* callous, but hey, you *will* have a chance to tackle the car seat again, won't you?"

Simon rested his forehead on the steering wheel and groaned.

"Can't win either way, can I?"

"Nope."

"I'll still take unloading the SUV, car seat and all."

"Why am I not surprised?"

Only after Simon had gone, promising to return promptly at two o'clock Sunday afternoon, did Kit have another chance to consider what words he might have spoken if Nathan hadn't awakened. She couldn't think of anything more that he would have to say to her. He'd told her about his final conversation with Lucy, and then he'd left it up to her to believe him or not. He would have had no reason to bring up the issue again.

In fact, she had begun to believe him, though she hadn't yet told him so. She still couldn't understand, and likely never would understand, her friend's reasoning. But she wasn't so unfair as to expect Simon to defend himself against something so esoteric, either.

Maybe he had only wanted to express, again, his hope that they could remain on amicable terms during the time it took for him and Nathan to bond. Yet Kit was sure she'd seen something more in the way Simon had looked at her, just as she'd felt something more in the way he'd gripped her hand.

Or had she only transferred her own heightened emotions on to him? And why were her emotions heightened, anyway?

Simon Gilmore had never been interested in her as anything more than a friend, actually *Lucy's* friend. And now she was Nathan's caregiver. Naturally he'd be interested in her in that respect. But only for as long as she was allowed to control his access to his son.

Once the court set aside her right to act as Nathan's guardian—or her right had been wrested from her—Simon would likely forget all about her. And the latter could happen as soon as Sunday afternoon.

What if Mitchell and Deanna Gilmore insisted on keeping Nathan with them at the ranch? Simon would go along with them, of course, and she'd have no choice but to do the same. She wouldn't even have her own vehicle there to facilitate a getaway.

She shouldn't have agreed to go out to the ranch with Nathan, she realized. But then Simon would have forced the issue and likely won anyway. He'd taken the first step in establishing his parental rights, and the ball was rolling now. Nothing would stop it as far as Kit could see because Nathan *was* Simon's son.

Simon could be as reassuring as he wanted to be. He could be kind and gentle toward her to gain her cooperation. But the end result would be the same, whether it happened in two days' time or two weeks or even two months. She was going to lose Nathan one way or another.

But almost as distressing to Kit—not to mention surprising in the pain that it caused her—was the knowledge that she was going to lose Simon, too. Not that he had ever actually been *hers* to lose. She'd entertained that fantasy years ago despite the growing attraction between him and Lucy. And she'd caused herself unnecessary pain and disappointment as a result. No, letting go of Nathan was going to be difficult enough. Forming any kind of attachment to Simon, knowing full well she'd have to let him go, as well, would be nothing short of stupid.

Someone as smart and successful as she'd already proven herself to be wouldn't make that kind of mistake. But intelligence and achievement didn't guarantee that one also had common sense. Sometimes you could want your dream to be a reality so much that you ignored the hard, cold facts of life.

Times like now, Kit thought ruefully, sitting in the rocking chair with Nathan on her lap, letting him turn the pages of a picture book. Times when you knew that facing the cold, hard facts of life would break your heart, and entertaining a fantasy seemed the only way to keep yourself together.

Chapter Eight

Simon drove the winding road from the ranch to Belle in a heightened state of anticipation on Sunday afternoon. He was looking forward to seeing his son again after a self-imposed interval of almost forty-eight hours. But having the opportunity to spend a little time with Nathan was only one reason for his exuberance. He was also going to spend a little time with Kit, and that accounted in equal measure for the excitement pulsing through him. The shy girl had become an alluring woman full of grace and charm. He wanted to get to know her better in every way he could.

Simon hadn't gone into town at all on Saturday. He had chosen instead to ride along the ranch's fence line with his father and Andy Connor, the ranch foreman, in a battered pickup truck, searching for and repairing gaps in the barb-wire. It wasn't that he'd preferred not to see Nathan and Kit again so soon. Rather he had thought it wise to give

Kit a little breathing room. He knew that she had to be feeling pressured already. Hovering like a vulture would only add to her stress.

No matter how focused he'd been on fence mending—and one had to stay focused when barbwire was involved—Simon had thought of little else but Nathan and Kit during his long hours of hard work. Yet he had limited himself to one short telephone call Saturday evening, ostensibly to advise Kit that his mother hoped she would agree to stay for Sunday dinner.

After only the slightest hesitation, Kit had agreed that Sunday dinner at the ranch would be fine with her. She had also reported without prompting that Nathan had been more demanding than usual that day—a real handful, actually—probably due to all the attention he'd gotten from them on Friday.

"He won't be happy in his playpen for very much longer," Kit had added. "I'm going to have to ask Sara to watch him mornings as well as afternoons starting on Monday. And I was really counting on her helping in the diner for the breakfast rush now that the tourists have started driving through town on their way to the park."

"How about if I help out with Nathan so Sara can work in the diner? That would give me a chance to see him every day and learn how to tend to his needs on my own, in an environment he's used to," he had suggested in reply.

Kit hadn't answered him immediately, giving Simon time to realize that for all the care he'd taken to keep his distance that day, he had just pushed her into yet another very uncomfortable corner. The hell of it was that he'd only wanted to help her out of a jam. But she likely hadn't thought of his offer in quite that way.

"That's probably a good idea," she'd admitted at last, an odd catch in her voice. "The sooner Nathan gets to know you and feel comfortable with you, the better for him…and for you, of course."

"I don't want to cause you any problems or run Sara out of a job," he'd hastened to say.

"No problem at all. Sara prefers working in the diner. I pay her the same hourly wage, regardless, but she can earn tips, too, waiting tables."

"Thanks for agreeing to stay for Sunday dinner."

"No problem there, either. I'd be eating diner leftovers otherwise, and I've had enough of those lately, thank you very much," she'd replied in a wry tone. Then she added after a moment's hesitation, "It's very kind of your parents to include me."

"They're really looking forward to seeing you as well as Nathan."

"We'll be ready at two o'clock."

Now driving down Belle's quiet, tree-lined Main Street, Simon noted that he'd timed his arrival at the Dinner Belle almost exactly right. He was a few minutes early—understandable under the circumstances—as he pulled to a stop in front of the diner and climbed out of the SUV.

The diner was closed as it had been on Sundays during Kit's mother's lifetime, too. Even during the summer months when hungry tourists would have packed the place—or maybe especially then—Dolores Davenport had believed in the benefits of having at least one day of rest. Simon was glad that Kit had maintained the tradition.

Running a place like the Dinner Belle, even with the help she had, plus caring for a busy two-year-old had to be exhausting for Kit. But she wasn't going to have to cope alone with Nathan anymore. He'd be there to help her, starting…well, today, actually. And he would be there for her until…until he gained full custody of his son and returned with him to Seattle and the life he'd made for himself there.

Considered in such blunt and basic terms, Simon's ultimate goal suddenly seemed to him not altruistic but selfish and unsparing. He had a right to raise his son, but he also had a responsibility to treat Kit fairly. She had taken Lucy's place in Nathan's life. He couldn't just cut her out because he had the law on his side. He didn't *want* to cut her out. He wanted…

The side door of the diner opened and Kit stepped outside, totally arresting his attention. She wore a slim, sleeveless, midcalf-length dress belted at her narrow waist. The pale peach color of it contrasted with her hair in a most becoming way. A single strand of pearls peeking from the dress's V-neck and matching pearl earrings added a touch of unexpected elegance, as did her thin-strapped sandals.

She looked not only more sophisticated, but also more attractive than Simon had ever seen her look in the past. She had always been a pretty girl, but now he saw that she had become a truly beautiful woman, graceful and self-assured, as she had every right to be.

Though she must have been aware of him as he stood by the SUV's front bumper, Kit didn't immediately acknowledge him with a glance or a wave of her hand.

Her attention was focused on the little boy walking along beside her, clinging to her hand and also clutching his teddy bear. Dressed in navy-blue shorts, a navy-and-green-striped polo shirt tucked in at the waist and miniature sandals, Nathan looked amazingly grown up.

Simon could hear the musical lilt of Kit's voice as she spoke to the child, but he couldn't make out her words. Nathan listened attentively, a serious look on his face. Then as Kit finally shifted her gaze to Simon and gestured in his direction, Nathan, too, looked his way. His eyes widened with surprise and a joyous smile lit his expression. Tugging at Kit's hand, he toddled forward, waving his bear and calling, "Dahee, Dahee, *Dahee...*"

"Hey, buddy, happy to see me again?"

Simon bent to pick up the child. Hands at his waist, he held him high for a moment as Nathan screeched with delight, then settled him securely in the crook of his arm.

"Seems so, doesn't it?" Kit paused a few feet away, her own smile not quite masking the weariness edging her eyes. "I'll get the car seat," she added, taking a step to turn away.

With a single stride, Simon caught up with her before she could slip away completely. He didn't want her to feel that he'd shut her out of the family unit he and Nathan made. Nor did he want her to think of him as an interloper encroaching on her territory.

In fact, he had wanted to reach out and hug her close as he held Nathan because he was equally happy to see her. More so, maybe, if the sudden pounding of his pulse was any indication. But she hadn't come close enough, and then she'd made as if to flee.

"You look really nice today," he said, halting her with a hand on her arm, his grip firm but gentle.

"Thank you," she replied after a long moment, then tipped her head in acknowledgment of his khaki shorts, black T-shirt and deck shoes. "You're not looking too shabby yourself—very summer in the city. Now, if you'll let me get the car seat..."

"Actually I have one," he said with a self-deprecating smile. "Borrowed from the ranch foreman. His youngest has outgrown it. He offered to let me use it so we wouldn't have to keep switching yours from one vehicle to another. He even showed me how to secure it with the same cocky attitude you did."

Kit didn't seem nearly as pleased, or impressed, as he'd expected her to be. She looked just the slightest bit dismayed, but then quickly covered her initial response with a slight smile.

"That was nice of him," she said, moving a step back to free her arm from his hold. "I'll just collect the diaper bag and my purse then while you get Nathan settled. You *will* still be here when I come back, won't you?"

Though she asked the question in a diffident tone, Simon sensed that she was seriously concerned. His first instinct was to grab her, give her a good shake and tell her in no uncertain terms that he had no intention of kidnapping his own child. But he was still holding Nathan, and Nathan was banging him gently on the chin with his teddy bear, and Kit's question was too ridiculous to rate anything but an equally ridiculous response.

"To be honest, I'd planned to leave you standing on the curb *after* I grabbed the diaper bag out of your hand. But now that you've coerced me into admitting it, I've obviously lost the element of surprise, haven't I?"

"Very funny," Kit muttered in an equally sarcastic tone.

She did, however, also have the good grace to blush as she turned away.

"Better grab a sweater—one for Nathan, too. It will be chilly later this evening."

"Already packed away in the diaper bag," she replied.

"Sure you can manage the straps on the car seat on your own?"

"I practiced all morning," he countered as he opened the back door of the SUV. "I'm practically an expert at car seats now."

"Yes, well…I'll believe *that* when I see it."

Kit had vowed that she wasn't going to start out Sunday afternoon in a prickly mood. Her best intentions were waylaid almost immediately, though. Not so much by what Simon said and did as by her skewed interpretation of his basically reasonable behavior.

Of course Nathan was happy to see Simon—probably fascinated by him, as well, since there hadn't been a man in his life till now. Simon was a new and very interesting addition to the little boy's life. He probably seemed like an overgrown playmate to Nathan—a playmate who also treated him with kindness and affection.

She was the one who chose to stand back as father and son greeted each other. They hadn't excluded her—she had excluded herself. Rather than allow that Simon could have his place in Nathan's life and she could have hers, she had gotten it into her head that Simon had replaced her in importance.

He had taken it upon himself to provide a car seat for the child, hadn't he? She'd bet he also had diapers and bottles, along with just about anything else required by a two-year-old boy, waiting for him at the ranch. That realization had quickly spawned another—she obviously wasn't needed, and thus obviously not wanted. In less than five minutes, Kit had gone from eager expectation to undisguised and irascible irritation, revealing her worst, and in hindsight, most irrational, fear.

Only when Simon made his comment about the diaper bag had Kit recognized just how outlandish her thought processes had become. Simon's main intention had been to enjoy spending time with Nathan, and with her, if she would allow it.

No one had forced him to invite her to the ranch. Had he not wanted to include her in the outing, he wouldn't have. And had he not wanted her to relax and enjoy the afternoon, he would have treated her in a polite but distant manner.

Sitting beside him in the front passenger seat of the SUV, hands clasped in her lap, Kit spent the first few minutes of the drive to the ranch silently adjusting her attitude. *She* was the one making the situation more difficult than it had to be. *She* was the one who assigned hurtfully underhanded motives to Simon's every word and deed when common sense should have told her none actually existed.

She would have only herself to blame if Simon decided he and Nathan would be better off without her disturbing and disrupting presence in their lives. All she had done so far was treat him like a villain—though he hadn't given her any reason to do so. He deserved so much better than that from her, and she knew it.

"You're awfully quiet," Simon ventured. "I hope you're not nervous about spending the afternoon at the ranch. We have a Gilmore family rule—absolutely no changing into werewolves on Sundays, especially when guests are present. You'll be safe until midnight, and I solemnly promise to have you back home again long before then."

"I deserved that, didn't I?" Kit glanced at Simon, offering him a wry smile.

"Yes, you most certainly did."

"I owe you an apology," she admitted before she could lose her nerve. "I haven't been very fair to you the past few days, and I'm sorry for that. I've held on to old beliefs about you—false beliefs, I now realize—and I've behaved badly toward you as a result.

"You said some things about Lucy on Friday, things that I've thought about a lot since then and that I have to admit are true. She did have a way of twisting the truth to suit her purposes. I don't know why she lied to you about Nathan one way and me another. I'm sure I never will. But I do know that you're not a mean, hurtful person, capable of harming a child. I also know you have Nathan's best interests at heart, just as I do, and because of that I hope we can at least try to be friends now, as well as in the future."

"That's what I've wanted all along, Kit. But you haven't exactly been making it easy," Simon pointed out, though in a kindly tone.

"Yes, I know, and again, I'm sorry. If you'll give me a chance, I promise I'll try to do better."

"You do know, don't you, that it's as important to me as it is to Nathan that you're a part of our…transition? We both need your help. You're an important part of his life, and that makes you an important part of my life, too."

"I appreciate that, Simon, and of course, I feel the same way about you. Anyone who matters in Nathan's life matters to me, too."

Kit didn't add that she understood her place, and thus her importance, was only temporary. She simply assumed that was what Simon meant when he said she was part of their transition. Inevitably they would go their separate ways, taking up again the lives they'd set aside, once that transition was made.

"Now that we've got that settled, do you think you'll be able to relax and enjoy the rest of the day?" To emphasize his request, he reached across the console and put a hand over hers. "You still seem a little tense."

"It's not like I'm a regular guest at the Double Bar S," she replied, her tone lighter and just a tad teasing as she referred to the ranch by the name that reflected its brand. "I'm trying to compose myself so that my demeanor will be appropriately ladylike upon our arrival."

"Oh, please." Simon snorted and shook his head. "It's a working cattle ranch, not a country estate. You've also been there several times already," he added, reminding her of the times he had invited her, along with Lucy, to a summer barbecue or a holiday party at his home.

Mitchell and Deanna Gilmore had always made her feel welcome, and she had always had a good time. But she hadn't been there for several years, and the circumstances were somewhat different now.

"I know, but I was always part of a crowd back then. I could fade into the woodwork and enjoy myself without attracting any attention. I'm not going to be able to do that today."

"You really think that's true—that you faded into the woodwork and didn't attract any attention?" Simon asked with obvious amazement.

"Of course it's true. I was a little brown mouse, shy and quiet. Lucy was the one who attracted attention. She was pretty and popular, the life of any party she attended."

"I *always* knew you were there," Simon said, suddenly sounding quite serious. "And I never once thought of you as a little brown mouse. You might not have been as flashy as Lucy, but your style was just as attractive in its own way.

You were so smart, too. But you weren't a snob—you were a really nice person. I admired you so much. I still do."

Kit stared at Simon for several moments, stunned speechless by the compliments he'd paid her. Then she shifted her gaze out the window again. She felt a nervous flutter in her stomach as she saw that they had turned onto the gravel road that led to the Gilmores' single-story ranch house built of wood and stone.

"That's very kind of you to say," she finally murmured.

"Nothing especially kind about it," Simon said, still pensive. "I just wish I'd realized sooner how important those qualities are and acted accordingly."

Again Kit looked at him, wondering what he meant. Granted, she had an idea, but it seemed too preposterous to be true. Before she could give it any more thought, though, Simon took a hand from the steering wheel and gestured toward the house.

"The welcoming committee awaits, quite eagerly if I'm not mistaken," he advised, postponing indefinitely any further discussion between them regarding past regrets.

Sure enough, Mitchell and Deanna Gilmore were on their way down the wide stone steps that led from the house's long covered porch to the stone walkway connecting the house to the drive that curved in front of it. Simon's mother wore a denim skirt and red sleeveless shirt knotted fashionably at her slender waist. His father was also dressed casually in neatly pressed jeans and a white knit shirt.

Kit noted that they held hands as if they were offering each other much-needed support. They looked both excited and uncertain. The effort they made to wait patiently until

Simon pulled to a stop was evident, as well, in the rigid way they stood.

Suddenly Kit wished she had encouraged Simon to take Nathan to the ranch on his own. She felt like an intruder, her presence there unnecessary, and despite what Simon had said, perhaps even unwelcome at such a private moment.

His parents were about to meet their grandson for the first time. How could they want a virtual stranger looking on from the sidelines during such an intensely emotional moment?

To her surprise, Simon took a moment to touch her lightly, reassuringly, on the shoulder after he switched off the SUV's engine.

"We're all glad you're here today," he said, as if aware of her inner turmoil. "I hope you are, too, because you are very, very welcome."

"Thank you," she replied, wanting more than anything to believe that what he said was true.

"Sit tight and let me show off my gentlemanly skills, okay?"

"Okay…"

Though she wasn't exactly sure what he meant, she was willing enough to find out.

Behind them, Nathan chattered excitedly, more than ready to be released from his car seat now that their ride seemed to be over.

"Hang on, buddy. It's one at a time, and Miss Kit is first," Simon advised the little boy, then opened the door of the SUV and stepped out.

Proving himself every bit a gentleman, Simon greeted his parents as he crossed to Kit's door. He opened it for her, offering her a supportive hand as she climbed out. He led her to the steps where his parents waited. "Mom, Dad, you remember Kit Davenport," he said.

Kit held out her hand to his mother, then his father, noting with relief how direct their gazes were, how firm their handshakes and how genuinely their smiles glowed with warmth as they responded to her quiet greeting.

"Thank you for coming today, Kit," Mitchell Gilmore said.

"Yes, thank you so much," Deanna Gilmore added. "We are so very glad that you accepted our invitation. We were sorry to hear about your mother's death, and Lucy's, when we returned to Belle a few weeks ago. And we really appreciate all you've done for Nathan. These past few months must have been very hard for you. I admire you so much for how well you've managed on your own."

Deanna Gilmore's sincerity was so apparent that Kit couldn't take offense. Nor could she point out that she hadn't cared for Nathan only out of a sense of duty. Simon's mother had meant to compliment her, and Kit responded with a few gracious words of thanks. To her relief, the real guest of honor then diverted their attention.

"Mom, Dad…this is Nathan. Nathan, meet your grandma and your grandpa," Simon said.

Looking at Simon as Mitchell and Deanna did, Kit saw the pride in his eyes as he gazed at his son, snuggled shyly against his shoulder, teddy bear gripped close for added security.

"Hey, young man," Mitchell said, his deep voice pitched low as he reached out tentatively and touched the little boy's cheek with a weathered hand.

Nathan offered the beginning of a smile to the tall, sil-

ver-haired man, then shifted his gaze to Simon's mother
as she spoke.

"Oh, Simon, he's beautiful," Deanna murmured, her
voice teary. "He reminds me so much of you at that age."
She paused a moment and glanced at Kit, then asked hopefully, "Do you think he'd let me hold him or would that
frighten him?"

"He only pretends to be shy," Kit replied. "Hey, Nathan,
come here a minute and give me a hug."

"Hug…hug…hug…"

The little boy laughed with delight as Kit took him
from Simon. Then he wrapped his chubby arms around her
neck, teddy bear still clutched in one little fist, and gave
her the hug she'd requested.

"Okay, now give Grandma a hug, too," she instructed
as she shifted Nathan to Deanna's waiting arms.

"Gahma?" he asked, gazing up at Simon's mother in
wide-eyed curiosity.

"Yes, precious boy, I'm your grandma," Deanna replied,
smiling despite the shimmer of tears in her eyes. "Can I
have a hug, too?"

"Hug…hug…hug…"

Nathan laughed again, batted his eyes flirtatiously at his
grandmother, then joyfully gave her a hug.

Kit had tears in her eyes, as well, as she watched Nathan bond with his grandmother and then, after a moment's
hesitation, his grandfather. Not used to being around many
men, he still seemed somewhat in awe of Mitchell
Gilmore, but the little boy needed only a little coaxing to
give him a hug, too.

Those first moments of sharing Nathan with Simon's
parents were bittersweet for Kit. She knew how much

she'd missed, growing up without a father. She wanted Simon to be a part of Nathan's life, just as she wanted Nathan to become a beloved part of Simon's entire family. Already, to her relief, that had plainly begun to happen. But at the same time, she felt yet again as if she'd been shifted off to the sidelines, and was on the outside looking in at a place she also longed to be.

Seeming to sense the battle she fought with her emotions, Simon moved to stand beside her, then slid a supportive arm around her shoulders. She didn't want to lean on him—didn't want to even tempt the thought that she could turn to him now, or any time in the future, for comfort and support.

But before she could stop herself, she shifted closer to him, touched by his sympathy and understanding. He knew how much Nathan meant to her—she'd made no secret of it. And he knew, as well, that she was willing to do whatever was best for the little boy no matter the cost to her personally. In an odd way, the fact that Simon could acknowledge her pain went a long way toward easing it as Nathan slipped away from her a little further.

"I've fixed up a room for Nathan with Simon's help, and Mitchell's," Deanna said, turning back to Kit with a hopeful smile. "Would you like to see it while the men start the grill? I wasn't sure if you'd prefer steak or chicken or fish so we're having all three."

"I'd love to see Nathan's room, and steak, chicken and fish all sound equally good to me," she answered graciously.

Aware that Deanna Gilmore was feeling her way as carefully as she was, Kit could finally begin to relax a little. They were allies, after all, and they had a common goal. Maybe one day they could be friends, as well.

Tired of being held and also anxious to explore his new surroundings, Nathan asked to be put down. When Mitchell had set him on his feet, he toddled over to Deanna and offered her his most charming smile.

"Well, little one, would you like to see your room, too?" she asked, holding out her hand to him.

"Gahma…"

He took Deanna's hand and gave it a tug, letting her know he had places to go and things to do at the ranch, and the sooner they got started, the better he'd like it.

"Smart boy," Simon said to Kit, making no effort at all to hide his pride as he gave her shoulder a gentle squeeze. "He already knows who the real softie is around here. She's going to have him spoiled rotten before the day's over, and enjoy every minute of it."

"That's what a grandmother does best," Deanna advised without apology. "Now go help your father with the grill while I give Kit and Nathan a tour of the house."

"Have fun," Simon said as he gave Kit's shoulder a last squeeze before releasing her.

"You, too," she replied with a grateful smile, then turned to follow his mother into the cool, quiet, tastefully yet comfortably furnished house the Gilmore family had called home for at least three generations.

Chapter Nine

The public areas of the Gilmore home—living room, dining room, kitchen, breakfast nook and den—looked much the same as Kit remembered them. She had never been in any of the bedrooms, but the one allotted to Nathan was light and bright and spacious enough to accommodate a baby bed, changing table, dresser and rocking chair, all obviously kept in storage since Simon's childhood. A small assortment of age-appropriate toys was scattered over the floor, immediately attracting the little boy's attention.

They allowed Nathan to play until Simon came to tell them the grill was ready. Then they took Nathan out to the patio, along with some of his new toys, so they could all be together while Mitchell tended the barbecue.

To Kit's relief, Deanna didn't quiz her about Lucy's behavior, or the choices she'd made, during the time they were alone together. She simply said again that she was sorry Lucy had died so tragically.

Simon's mother seemed more interested in the present than the past, and that was fine with Kit. She wanted to know all about Nathan, including details of his likes and dislikes and his daily schedule. Kit gladly answered all of her questions. She also enjoyed hearing about all the ways in which Nathan's behavior mimicked Simon's when he was the same age.

It was both amusing and endearing to think of Simon refusing to eat green peas with the same unhappy face that Nathan displayed, and to know that Simon, too, had carried around a stuffed teddy bear. Like Kit, Deanna had once lived in dread of losing that bear, and she still had it tucked away in a box, wrapped in tissue paper and fond memories.

By the time Simon had come to invite them out to the patio, Kit felt as if Deanna Gilmore had most definitely become her friend as well as her ally. Not only had Simon's mother treated her with kindness and consideration, she had also deferred to her wishes where Nathan was concerned.

She asked if she could change his diaper when he began to fuss. She asked if Kit wanted him to have milk or juice when he asked for a drink. She asked if a cookie would spoil his dinner. In fact, she behaved as if Kit were Nathan's mother, not merely his temporary guardian. And she did so not with resentment, but rather with such regard that it warmed Kit's heart.

The rest of the afternoon and early evening progressed in much the same manner. Mitchell and Deanna's goodwill and camaraderie toward her was evident in all they said and did.

Kit had felt genuinely welcome—as genuinely welcome as she could feel under the circumstances, she amended as the evening shadows began to lengthen. Standing alone in the den, looking out the French doors to the patio and the sloping lawn beyond where Simon's parents walked with Nathan, each holding one of his little hands, she acknowledged a tiny nudge of doubt that remained despite her best efforts at banishment.

Watching them, she had no doubt at all that they would do whatever was necessary to gain her goodwill if that's what it took to have access to their grandson prior to the court's ruling that would grant Simon custody.

It was obvious that they would love and cherish Nathan as much as they'd always loved and cherished Simon. Kit was glad of that, of course. They were his family, after all, his own flesh and blood. But Kit also knew they couldn't possibly love and cherish Nathan more than she did.

He had been her godson before Lucy's death, and since then she'd come to think of him as her own child, as dear to her as any child born of her body would be. Having to give him up to people who loved him didn't make the giving up any easier. Nor did it even begin to soothe the ache already blossoming in her heart.

Caught unaware by thoughts she'd tried to keep from her mind that day, Kit felt the prickle of tears in her eyes. The last thing she wanted to do just then was cry. But still, the first tear trickled down her cheek, followed by another and another. She tried to brush them away with her hand, tried to take a deep, calming breath. But unexpectedly the breath turned into a sob triggered by a soul-deep sorrow she could no longer ignore.

Pressing the heels of her hands to her eyes, Kit willed herself to get a grip, only to sob again.

"Kit? Are you okay?"

Simon's voice, laced with concern, rumbled somewhere

close behind her. His sudden presence there in the den startled her, but not enough to stem the flow of her tears. She hated the fact that he had caught her in a moment of such distress, weeping inconsolably. Yet she couldn't seem to find the strength to pull herself together.

"Go away," she pleaded, keeping her back to him. "Just please, *please* go away."

"Not likely," he muttered, suddenly close behind her, his hands warm against the bare skin of her shoulders.

"I'm okay. Really, I am. Just having a…a…"

What? Kit wondered. A momentary lapse in good manners, or more likely, a complete and total breakdown?

Guest found sobbing her heart out after perfectly lovely day hosted by perfectly lovely people who—oh by the way—had more right to her child than she did. Men in white coats called to the scene and asked to haul her away.

She should have laughed at her foolishness—would have laughed if the truth hadn't hurt so much.

Although the heightening of her emotions could have been the result of the way Simon tenderly turned her to face him, then held her close, stroking a gentle hand over her hair as he murmured soothing words, causing fresh tears to spill from her eyes.

"It's all right," he said over and over again. "It's going to be all right. I promise you it will."

Kit wanted to tell him that he couldn't promise her any such thing—not if he intended to take Nathan from her. But the way he held her, the way he touched her hair, the way he spoke words meant only to soothe her, worked some strange kind of magic on her, warming her heart, settling the distress in her soul. She found herself wanting to believe him, needing to trust the sincerity of his vow.

Finally she managed to gather her runaway emotions. The last of her tears spent, her breathing again steady, she wiped a hand over her face, then groped in the pocket of her dress for a tissue so she could blow her nose.

"Better?" Simon asked, still holding her close.

"A little," she replied, taking a careful step back, then looking up at him with watery eyes. "Sorry. I don't know what came over me. I was having a really nice time…."

"I think I have a pretty good idea."

Meeting her gaze, Simon rubbed a thumb along her cheekbone, gathering a last, lingering teardrop.

"Well, I'm fine now. Just fine."

She looked away from him, afraid that she would cry again if she didn't.

"Are you, Kit? Are you really fine?"

He touched a hand to her chin and turned her face so that she couldn't avoid his tender, probing gaze.

"Yes…no…I don't know…" she muttered, her voice as beseeching as the glance she cast his way.

"Ah, Kit, I never meant to hurt you."

"I know that, Simon. I do know that."

She made to turn away again, but he wouldn't let her go. Instead he slid his hand from her shoulder to the back of her neck, tipped her face up with a thumb under her jaw, bent his head and kissed her on the mouth.

Not a tiny, tender kiss offered friend to friend, but a long, slow, deep, searching kiss. A kiss that had its root in hot desire, not cool comfort or ambiguous affection. A kiss so unlike the one he'd given her that day in the diner that they could have been two totally different people now than they had been then.

But that was true. So much had changed between them

in the short time that had passed since he'd come back into her life. This kiss, though—this kiss that she returned with a fervor that left her slightly stunned—this kiss was something else altogether. Something that exhilarated her and scared her half to death, something that treaded near to the impossible, yet offered a first taste of hope where hope shouldn't have existed.

She was the one to finally break away, shoving her hands hard against Simon's chest as she took a determined step back, just as she had at the diner. Surprised, he released her immediately, but Kit sensed that he was reluctant to let her go.

"That wasn't a good idea," she said, struggling for composure.

She refused to meet his steady, questioning gaze, choosing instead to focus on a point somewhere over his left shoulder. She didn't want to see the sympathy that must be in his eyes. Nor did she want to face the fact that he had probably only meant to be kind while she had turned the kiss into something else. Something inappropriate, something…sexual….

"You're probably right," he agreed after a long, silent moment, causing her to feel even more embarrassed until he added with a wry chuckle, "although kissing you felt pretty darn good to me, and you didn't seem to mind it all that much. But my folks *are* heading this way. I don't really mind if they catch me kissing you, but I have a feeling it would make *you* uncomfortable, and I don't want to do that to you."

"Yes, it would," Kit acknowledged, her pride somewhat restored by his gallantry. "But that's not the only reason kissing you wasn't a good idea. The situation I'm in is complicated enough, not to mention painful enough, for me already. "

"It doesn't have to be," Simon replied, a speculative look in his eyes. "It's the…complications that are making the situation painful, not only for you, but also for me."

"So how do you suggest we unravel the mess we're in?" she asked. "Are you going to relinquish your parental rights and let me adopt Nathan the way I'd planned to do?"

"That's one thing I'm definitely *not* going to do," he stated, his tone firm yet gentle.

"No surprise there," Kit said, allowing more than a hint of sarcasm to edge her voice as she turned away from him at last.

Simon's parents were on the patio now, walking slowly toward the French doors. Not wanting to face them again until she'd had a chance to wash her face and repair her makeup, she headed for the hall bath.

"He's my son, Kit. I never intentionally abandoned him, and I'm not going to abandon him now."

"I know, Simon." She paused a moment in the hallway to look back at him, her gaze steady. "I know, and I understand, but that doesn't make it hurt any less."

Again she turned away and this time he let her go without offering any further reply.

They had come full circle. Reality had given way momentarily to a fantasy solution that only seemed to be in Simon's mind. Then reality had come crashing through again. All triggered by a single kiss sparked by emotions—*her* emotions—allowed to run out of control.

Simon had always been the type to favor a peaceful solution to any problem. More often than not he had allowed Lucy to have her way just to avoid a fight. But there was

no peaceful solution to the custody problem they faced—
at least none that would be equally acceptable to her as
well as Simon.

He already had the upper hand. He didn't have to com-
promise to get what he wanted. He wasn't the kind of man
who would hurt anyone intentionally. But if hurting her
was the price he had to pay to get his son, she knew that
he would do it.

By the time Kit returned to the den, Simon's parents
were also there along with Nathan. The little boy's bedtime was less than an hour away, and understandably he
had begun to fuss, clutching his teddy bear and sucking
a thumb. Looking over at her, Simon suggested that they
head back to Belle, and much relieved, she readily
agreed.

They made their farewells as Simon secured Nathan in
his car seat. Kit received hugs from both Mitchell and Deanna as well as an invitation to return again with Nathan
as soon as she could, if not one evening during the week,
then definitely the following weekend.

Kit promised to let Simon's mother know when to expect them once she'd had a chance to check her schedule. Granted, she had no plans, but she wasn't quite
ready to commit to another visit with them until she'd
had a little time to regroup emotionally. She knew that
Simon's parents meant well, but that didn't make it any
easier to accept the fact that one day soon she would
have to take Nathan to the Double Bar S and go home
all alone.

Simon was very quiet on the drive back to town. Though
Kit couldn't see the expression on his face well enough in
the gathering darkness to judge his mood, he didn't seem

to be angry. Having a conversation would have been hard to do, as well, with Nathan fussing and squirming in his car seat. Still she found his silence slightly unnerving.

He seemed to have something on his mind that he wasn't inclined to share with her. She couldn't blame him for holding back. She'd been snappy and sarcastic the last time he'd tried to talk to her. But she didn't like feeling that he was plotting against her.

Though what he could be plotting to do, that would be worse than taking Nathan from her, she couldn't begin to imagine.

By the time they reached the Dinner Belle, Nathan was wailing inconsolably and Kit had a splitting headache. She wasted no time hopping out of the SUV when Simon pulled to a stop at the curb. She made short work of releasing the little boy from his car seat while Simon stood by with the diaper bag in hand.

"Do you want me to come upstairs with you and help get Nathan settled for the night?" he asked politely.

"No, thanks. I can manage on my own."

Actually, it would have been nice to have Simon's help, but she was feeling just perverse enough to deny herself the comfort of his company completely out of hand.

"He sounds pretty upset about something."

"He's just tired, and when he gets tired, he gets cranky," she explained impatiently.

She couldn't allow his concern to soften her independent stance even a little.

"Well, then, I guess I'll see you tomorrow morning," Simon said, then hesitated when she glanced at him in confusion. "Unless you've changed your mind about letting me look after Nathan for you."

In fact, Kit had forgotten about his offer to take care of Nathan, but she didn't say as much.

"Yes, of course, tomorrow morning…see you then."

"What time would you like me to be here?"

"Seven o'clock?"

"Okay. I'll be here at seven."

He let her take the diaper bag from him with her free hand, but insisted on taking her key and unlocking the side door of the diner for her.

"I'm really glad you came today, Kit," he said as the door swung open and he handed back her key.

"I had a very nice time. Please thank your parents for me again when you get home."

"I will."

He hesitated another moment as if waiting for her to say something more. Then before she could turn away completely, he caught her arm, ducked his head and kissed her on the cheek.

"Good night, Kit, and good night to you, too, little buddy."

He gave Nathan a quick kiss, as well, then let her go.

Touched by his tenderness, Kit was tempted to call him back, to invite him upstairs and accept the solace he seemed so ready to offer her. But she had behaved in a silly and regrettable way once already that day.

"See you tomorrow," she said as he crossed the sidewalk to his vehicle.

In reply he lifted his hand in a salute, but he didn't look back at her again. Biting off the words that would have had him turning back to join her in the doorway, Kit watched as he slid behind the steering wheel and started the engine.

Her cheek seemed to burn where his lips had lingered

only a second or two, and in her heart a longing she couldn't deny began to swell. Only when the taillights of the SUV disappeared from sight as it rounded a corner did she finally climb the stairs to the apartment.

Suddenly subdued, Nathan rested his head on her shoulder and whimpered softly.

"Dahee…" he said, sounding no less bereft than Kit felt. "Dahee…Dahee?"

"He'll be back tomorrow, sweetie. I promise," she assured him, and herself. "Tomorrow…"

Chapter Ten

Leaving Kit standing with Nathan at the side door of the Dinner Belle Diner Sunday night was no easy task for Simon. He'd had thoughts to share with her, ideas to pursue. But she had so obviously wanted him gone that he knew it would be best if he went along with her wishes.

What he'd wanted to suggest to her had the potential to be of great consequence, not only to both of them, but to Nathan, as well. He hadn't wanted to risk having her dismiss the possibility he intended to present simply because she was annoyed with him. He wanted her to be in a receptive mood when he gave voice to his thoughts, although even then there was a good chance she'd think he was crazy. In fact, *he* had thought he was crazy when the unlikely scheme first came to him.

Seeing Kit crying quietly as she looked out at his parents, walking with Nathan on the back lawn, Simon had known at once the reason for her tears. He had also known that he was responsible. In the past six months she'd lost her mother and her best friend, and soon he would be taking custody of the little boy she so obviously loved.

Simon had hated being the one to cause Kit such anguish, but as he'd put his arms around her and tried to comfort her, he hadn't seen that he had any other choice. He was Nathan's father. Not only did he have a legal right to his child, but also a moral duty.

Beyond that, his son had claimed a huge piece of his heart. His love for Nathan had come swiftly, easily, over the space of a few days, but Simon knew it was also deep and abiding. No matter what challenges lay ahead, Simon had vowed that he would always be there for his precious little boy.

Holding Kit close in his arms, Simon had acknowledged that there was no way the two of them could be a part of Nathan's daily life—24/7—unless, of course, they married.

He had been momentarily stunned by the audacity of such a thought. He liked Kit and there was an undeniable attraction brewing between them, but he wasn't in love with her. And most of the time, she didn't even seem to *like* him.

Yet when she'd looked at him, the almost palpable pain he's seen in her teary eyes had seared him with the force of an arrow shot straight through his heart. He hadn't been able to stop himself from kissing her then. The urge to soothe her had been too great for him to resist.

But another urge, an urge prompted by physical desire, man for woman, possessive as well as protective, had grabbed a hold of him in the instant after he'd put his mouth on hers. And Kit had responded in a way that had astonished him, at first, then seemed not quite so surprising, after all.

They had always known each other, albeit at a distance, growing up as they had in Belle. And spending time together with Lucy, they had become good friends. But Lucy had always stood between them, until now. Gone, through no fault of theirs, she had left them a legacy—a shared legacy in her son, Nathan. Not intentionally, of course, since she had lied to him as well as to Kit.

Still, he and Kit had already begun to form an alliance for Nathan's benefit. And to Simon's way of thinking, the kiss they had shared, especially the unexpected passion of it, had seemed to signal that a major shift in the initial course of their relationship had become a very real possibility.

No matter what Kit said about complications making for a painful situation between them, she had liked kissing him as much as he had liked kissing her—he couldn't deny the thought of having Kit in his bed was appealing. That was an incredibly strong and simple foundation on which to build something more, something permanent. They had a basic respect for each other, as well, and shared a mutual devotion to Nathan. Couples often married with a lot less going for them than that.

For his part, Simon had been too busy for more than casual dating the past three years. After Lucy, that had been enough for him. On a less positive note, however, he admitted that Kit might have a significant other in her life already. He found that hard to believe, though. He would have never allowed a woman he loved to cope alone with the death of her mother and her best friend, then the care of a two-year-old and the running of a small-town diner.

Any man who would do that to Kit wasn't worth the breath she'd have to draw to tell him to get lost.

But then, he hadn't been in town a week yet, Simon acknowledged as he drove back to the ranch. He couldn't assume he knew the score where Kit Davenport was concerned. He was going to make it his business to find out as soon as possible, though.

He'd also have to give a lot more thought to the pros and cons of marrying Kit—roll the idea around in his mind while he bided his time with her. The paternity test results wouldn't be available for at least two weeks. He'd be with Kit and Nathan daily until then, helping out with the little boy. He would have an opportunity to determine how he really felt about her as well as how she felt about him.

He wasn't about to push Kit into something she didn't honestly want to do. Nor was he going to make a commitment he wasn't fully prepared to keep. But he wasn't going to ignore the potential of what suddenly seemed to be a workable solution, either.

What was that old saying—faint heart never won fair lady?

Maybe if he'd challenged Lucy instead of taking her at her often-dubious word, she would have told him the real truth about Nathan. He couldn't change what he'd done in the past, but he could—and would—avoid making a similar mistake with Kit.

"Simon…you're right on time," Kit said, her tone cool and businesslike as she opened the apartment door to him at exactly seven o'clock on Monday morning.

Down in the diner, the first customers of the day were already trickling in, getting ready to enjoy breakfast thanks to the efforts of George in the kitchen and Bonnie and Sara's efficiency waiting tables. Bonnie had been the one to wave him upstairs when he'd first arrived, her smile as assessing as it was welcoming.

"I'm always on time," he admitted with a wry, hopefully reassuring smile. "I'm not sure if it's a blessing or a curse."

"Today it's definitely a blessing," Kit assured him.

She didn't return his smile before she turned and headed briskly for the kitchen. Though she was neatly dressed in jeans and a white knit shirt, she looked not only tired, but just a tad frazzled, as well.

"We're running late," she continued. "Nathan's still in his pajamas, still in his high chair and still eating breakfast. Or rather, smearing his breakfast all over everything within his reach, including himself. He's a little cranky today, but he's not running a fever. I don't think he's ill. He's probably still worn out from all the excitement yesterday."

Following Kit into the kitchen, Simon spied the mess Nathan had made with his oatmeal and mashed banana, and was more than half tempted to run for cover. He stood in the doorway a long moment and wondered what he'd gotten himself into.

Then he realized that each time he'd seen Nathan during the past week, the little boy had been scrupulously clean, neatly dressed and in a relatively good mood—all due to Kit's loving care. He had romanticized parenthood because so far he'd been at a distance from routine childcare. Up close and personal as he was today he could see that raising a child involved a lot of hard work. But it could also be the most fulfilling work any parent could do.

"Dahee…Dahee…Dahee," Nathan crowed, banging his spoon on the tray of his high chair.

The scowl on his little oatmeal-covered face changed to a delighted smile, and he squirmed in his seat, eager to be released.

"Hey, buddy, it's good to see you, too," Simon said, finally moving into the kitchen. "Let's get you out of your high chair."

"Wait a minute," Kit said. Catching him by the arm, she held out a wet washcloth. "You'd better wipe him off as best you can before you let him loose or there will be oatmeal and banana all over everything in the apartment."

"Oh, yeah…good idea." He offered her a sheepish smile. "Obviously I have a lot to learn."

"You have no idea," Kit replied, still unwilling, or unable, to offer him more than a distracted glance.

"But I bet you're going to change that real soon, though, aren't you?"

"I only have time to run through the basics to get you started. He probably needs to have his diaper changed. I've left a stack of them on the changing table in his room along with a container of baby wipes. I've also set out fresh clothes for him. I'd prefer that you give him milk, not juice, if he's thirsty, and if he seems hungry about ten o'-clock, which he probably will since he didn't eat much of his cereal, he can have another half of a banana or a small bowl of applesauce. I'll be back sometime between eleven-thirty and twelve with lunch. He should nap after that until two or two-thirty. If you have questions, give a holler down the steps and I'll come up, okay?"

"Okay," Simon agreed.

He wasn't sure why Kit had adopted such a condescending tone. But considering her attitude, he did know that he'd have to be downright desperate before he admitted that he couldn't handle one small boy on his own for part of a day.

Finally she met his gaze as she paused on her way to the kitchen doorway, and Simon understood at last why she seemed so hostile. She knew that she was going to have to trust him with Nathan eventually—the court would order it whether she cooperated or not. But that didn't mean she believed he was responsible enough, or capable enough, to look after his son on his own, either now or in the future.

Until he proved that he could handle any, and all, problems that arose while Nathan was in his care, Kit was going to worry, and that worry was going to be reflected in her manner toward him.

"You're sure you'll be all right with him?" she asked. "He can be a real handful when he wants to be."

"I think I'll be able to manage, but if I run into any problems I can't solve on my own, you won't be far away," he assured her.

"He may cry when I leave."

"Me, too," Simon said, unable to stop himself from grinning at her.

That turned out to be a good thing. Kit's look of concern eased noticeably, and though her own smile was only fleeting at best, she no longer appeared to be quite so troubled by the prospect of leaving Nathan alone with him.

"I'll be back at eleven-thirty."

"See you then."

Simon managed rather well during his first morning on his own with his son. He changed diapers, dressed the little boy, read to him from the assortment of picture books on the shelf in his room. Together he and Nathan built block towers and rolled small plastic cars and trucks along imaginary roads, making engine noises much to the little boy's delight.

Simon was actually surprised when Kit called out a greeting, announcing her return, as promised, at eleven-thirty. The time had flown by much faster than he'd expected.

"Did he cry after I left?" she asked as Nathan ambled across the living room toward her, waving his teddy bear and chortling with glee.

"Not a single tear," Simon reported with a newly confident smile, following after his son. He relieved Kit of the carryout containers she'd brought with her so she could bend down and give the little boy a hug. The delicious aromas wafting from the containers made his mouth water in anticipation. "I can also say quite proudly that I didn't cry, either."

She glanced up at him, seeming a little friendlier than she had earlier, though a frown still furrowed her forehead.

"No major problems, then?"

"Not a one. No minor problems, either. We managed two diaper changes, off with pajamas and on with jeans, T-shirt, socks and shoes, storybooks, toys and a banana snack without a hitch."

"Well, good for you," Kit said with the barest hint of a smile as she took Nathan by the hand and turned toward the kitchen. "We'd better eat before the food gets cold."

"Yeah, right."

To Simon's disappointment, Kit made no move to hug *him*. Though he considered himself equally worthy, he kept the thought to himself. She was probably so used to the work and worry of childcare that it likely hadn't crossed her mind that he might need a pat on the back after only some four hours on the job.

"I brought meat loaf, macaroni and cheese, and green beans, but if you'd rather have something else, you can go down and ask George to fix you a plate from today's menu."

"The Dinner Belle's meat loaf has always been one of my favorites," Simon assured her.

"Yes, I thought it was, and since George is cooking today, not me, it's as good as my mother used to make it."

Kit put Nathan in his high chair as Simon set the containers on the table, then took silverware from one of the drawers and glasses from a cabinet.

"Tea?" he asked.

"Yes, please."

"Are you saying you're not much good in the kitchen?" he asked in a teasing tone, filling their glasses.

"I can manage in a pinch, but I don't have the patience my mother had, plus she trained George. He really wanted to learn to cook. I can't say I did. I was content waiting tables and working the cash register. It was more fun to me being out with the customers than slaving over a hot stove."

"Dolores enjoyed doing both jobs, didn't she?"

"She *loved* doing everything necessary to keep the Dinner Belle Diner running smoothly," Kit replied. "That's why I hate the thought of closing the place. But I don't want to devote the rest of my life to keeping it open, either. I want to go back to Seattle and finish my graduate work. My advisor has offered me a teaching assistantship in the fall, and the people who have been subletting my apartment will be moving out at the end of July. I keep hoping I'll have a buyer for the diner by then. But if I don't..."

She looked away, her frown deepening as he set their glasses on the table and they sat down to eat.

"Will you be okay financially if you can't sell the Dinner Belle by the end of the summer?"

Simon was hesitant about prying too deeply into something so personal, yet he was also concerned about Kit's well-being. Coping with her mother's illness, then caring for Nathan the past few months could have easily drained her funds.

"I'm only asking because I'd be happy to help you out," he added when she didn't answer him immediately. "The least I should do is reimburse you for the money you've spent on Nathan."

"I don't really need your money, Simon, and I refuse to be bought," she replied, her voice tight, her chin tipped at a defensive angle. "I've been perfectly capable of taking care of myself and Nathan without the Gilmore family's charity. I don't expect to be reimbursed for anything I've done for him. I love him as if he were my own son, which, of course, he isn't, as you keep reminding me."

The fierce look in her eyes, coupled with her harsh, defensive tone, took Simon totally by surprise.

"It wasn't my intention to do that," he protested, only then aware of how easy it had been for her to misconstrue his motives. "And I certainly wasn't trying to buy you. I just don't want you to end up in debt or anything because of all you've done for Nathan."

"Well, I won't," she said with an air of finality he knew better than to ignore. "So there's no need for you to worry about it, okay?"

"Okay, I won't worry about it," he shot back, mentally throwing up his hands in defeat.

Why did every conversation he had with her have to end in acrimony? Was he really as loutish and insensitive—not to mention clueless and irresponsible—as she made him feel?

Each time he thought he was making progress with Kit, each time he dared to assume he'd proven he wasn't her enemy, she seemed to make a point of advising him otherwise. He was running out of ways to convince her that he really was one of the good guys. More importantly, he had begun to think that it was a waste of breath to keep trying.

He could direct his energy toward something more rewarding than spinning his wheels with her. He could cut out the friendly overtures, he could stop going out of his way to defend himself, and accept that they'd never be friends.

He could, *would*, deep-six all the thoughts he'd had about marrying her, too. Obviously, he hadn't been thinking straight when he'd come up with that ridiculous idea. Taking into account how determined she was to disapprove of everything he said or did, he knew that any relationship they had would continue to be hostile. How good would that be for Nathan, or for him?

Still, as Simon watched Kit clean off the tray of Nathan's high chair, her movements brisk, her mouth set in a grim line, he experienced a pang of longing so intense he had to forcibly stifle a rueful groan. He had never been a brute at heart, but oh, how he wanted just then to grab her and kiss her until she had no choice but to end her war against him.

"I have to get back to the diner," she advised him curtly,

dragging him from a rather pleasant reverie. "You'll need to put Nathan down for a nap within the next thirty minutes or so. Otherwise he'll want to sleep later into the afternoon and I'll have a hard time getting him to bed tonight. Do you think you'll be able to manage okay?"

Have it your way, then, Simon thought with an inward sigh. He was done trying to behave like a nice guy when she insisted on condescending to him at every opportunity.

"I'm not stupid, Kit, and I'm certainly not helpless. I managed just fine this morning. I'll manage just fine this afternoon," he said, mimicking her tone as he gathered the remains of his lunch. "Don't give either one of us another thought. We'll be just fine without you."

He heard her draw a startled breath as he crossed to the sink, and felt her gaze on him when he opened the refrigerator to retrieve one of the bottles she'd prepared. But he didn't acknowledge her with so much as a glance.

"Well, okay, then. I'll be back after we close at three o'-clock," she said in a surprisingly meek tone.

"I was thinking I'd take Nathan to the park for an hour or two after his nap. I'll have him home again by five at the latest."

No asking permission, he'd decided. Just a little advisory of what he intended to do with his son that afternoon.

Several seconds of highly charged silence followed his announcement. He would have liked to see the look on her face, but he kept his back to her as he slotted the bottle into the warmer on the counter.

"Fine," she said at last, her voice wrapped grimly around an agreement that wasn't really.

Simon ignored her unspoken expectation that he not only respond to, but also act upon, her reproach. She hesitated a few moments longer, murmured a few quiet words to Nathan, then stalked out of the kitchen, through the apartment and slammed the apartment door on her way out.

Simon didn't feel especially good about their altercation, but neither did he feel especially bad. He simply resigned himself to the fact that he'd done what he could with Kit. He had tried to be her friend and ally. Hell, he had seriously considered being even more than that to her. But she'd shown him every way she could that she wasn't interested.

Alone in the apartment, with Nathan asleep, the kitchen tidied and a load of Nathan's clothes in the washing machine—an initiative he'd taken upon himself—Simon switched on the television, then switched it off again after a few minutes of channel surfing. He wished he'd thought to bring his laptop computer, not to mention his camera, with him, but he hadn't anticipated having a couple of hours to himself while his son slept.

Technically he was on vacation, but he'd begun to think it might be interesting to write an article for the paper detailing his personal experience with unexpected fatherhood. He usually wrote about interesting people doing interesting things in interesting places. He'd never turned the focus on himself, but then, his life had been fairly mundane until now.

His editor might very well pass on the idea, but Simon wouldn't mind having a written record of how he'd first gotten to know his son. He wanted photographs of the little boy, as well, but until now, he'd had too many other things on his mind to begin a chronicle of Nathan's childhood.

Someday Nathan would ask about the past, about his

mother and likely about Kit if she remained a part of their lives. Here was a way he could answer honestly about how he'd found his son and how much the discovery had meant to him.

He would just jot down some notes while Nathan slept, Simon decided, going to the kitchen to get the pad of paper Kit kept by the telephone. He'd start a rough draft and add to it each day. That way he'd have something to occupy his mind. Maybe then he wouldn't think so much about Kit. Or about the effect she had on him.

Not that he could banish her completely from his thoughts or from the pages he wrote. She would always be there, but held at a distance, if not physically, then emotionally, until he could take Nathan home with him.

Just a few more weeks at the most, and he wouldn't have to deal with Kit Davenport unless he wanted to. Considering all he'd been through with her the past few days, that prospect should be appealing. Sadly though, that fact gave Simon no real comfort—no real comfort at all.

Chapter Eleven

She had finally done it, Kit admitted Wednesday afternoon as she gave the counter in the diner a final swipe with a damp cloth. She had finally alienated Simon so completely that she had little hope of ever being able to remedy the situation.

She had been in a truly unpleasant mood when he'd arrived at the diner Monday morning—no two ways about it. She had never functioned well on less than eight hours of sleep. She'd gotten maybe two hours tops Sunday night, and then only in snatches, solely because of her inability to put thoughts of Simon's passionate kiss out her mind.

She'd had only herself to blame for her exhaustion, yet Simon had quickly become the culprit. Everything he'd said, everything he'd done—no matter how innocent or well intentioned—had rubbed her the wrong way. Not only because she'd been bone-weary, though that had been a contributing factor. But she had also been on the brink of taking a step that would bring her that much closer to the moment when she would have to let Nathan go for good.

Kit had known how important it was for the little boy to bond with Simon. She had known, too, that loving Nathan as she did, she had to facilitate that bonding to the best of her ability. Only then could she ensure that the transfer of custody wouldn't upset Nathan in any way.

But actually having to leave Nathan alone with Simon, not to mention witnessing how well they managed on their own without her, had all but torn her heart out. Simon had taken over Nathan's care so efficiently, and Nathan had seemed so content to be with him, that for the first time in her life Kit couldn't help but feel dispensable.

Then, to have Simon offer to *pay* her for her services—Kit had never been so insulted by anything anyone had ever said to her. She didn't want, nor did she need, his charity—as she'd told him in no uncertain terms. More than that, though, she had been appalled by the assumption he so easily seemed to make that she'd cared for Nathan only to benefit financially—as if her love for the little boy hadn't been obvious to him, or perhaps, casually shuffled aside to relieve his own conscience.

So upset had she been, and so full of self-pity, that she'd snapped at him angrily without really considering first that his offer might have been made out of genuine concern for her. By the time she'd realized that had been the real reason he'd mentioned money, the damage to their relationship had already been done. Two days later, that damage still seemed to be irreparable.

Since Monday afternoon, Simon had taken to treating her exactly the same way she'd treated him. He was excruciatingly polite, of course, but very direct. He no longer initiated any amusing repartee, nor did he offer her any teasing grins or even any kindly comments. His answers to any questions she dared to ask were blunt and business-like, his own questions equally short and to the point.

He still deferred to her wishes regarding most aspects of Nathan's care. But he didn't ask her permission before taking his son on an outing. He presented his plan for the day, then waited wordlessly for her to object, which, of course, she didn't dare to do.

He'd begun by taking Nathan to the park to play each afternoon following his nap. Yesterday he and Nathan had also gone to the Western-wear store on the outskirts of town so Simon could buy the little boy his first pair of cow-boy boots. And today, instead of having lunch with her in the apartment—not exactly a convivial meal, she had to admit—he'd taken Nathan to a fast-food restaurant with an indoor play area similar to the one they'd stopped at in Missoula. He'd had the little boy home in time for his nap, but then they'd left again to go to the park thirty minutes ago.

Kit knew she should be glad to have a little time to relax on her own after the busy day she'd had at the diner. Just as she should be glad that Simon had bought Nathan his first pair of boots and remembered how much he enjoyed jumping into the pool of plastic balls at the play land. But all she felt as she finished cleaning up the diner's long, nar-row counter was lonely and left out.

"All done in the kitchen," Bonnie announced, breezing through the doorway. "Need any help out here?"

"I'm all done here, too," Kit said.

"We sure had a crowd today—at breakfast *and* at lunch.

Lots of tourists stopping in town on their way to the park. Several of the families I served said they'd been coming here for years. They were sorry to hear about your mother."

"I heard the same from some of the customers I served," Sara commented, joining Kit and Bonnie by the counter. "The tips have been really good, too. Thanks so much for letting me help out in the diner, Kit."

"I'm glad to have you both here. I couldn't manage otherwise. Now if I could just find somebody who wanted to buy the place…." Kit shrugged and shook her head. "I'm beginning to think that's not going to happen."

"Don't give up hope just yet," Bonnie advised. "There was an older couple in here today. They looked really familiar to me, but they're not locals. I asked if they'd been here before, and it turned out they've been Dinner Belle Diner regulars most summers for the past ten years. They're from Texas and they've recently retired, but they're not real happy about it. They've been thinking about buying a small business. I mentioned that you had the diner up for sale, and they looked really interested. I told them you had the place listed with Mountain View Realtors."

"Oh, Bonnie, thank you, thank you, *thank you*," Kit said, giving her friend a hug.

"I meant to tell you earlier, but we were so busy, I forgot. Maybe something will come of it, but then again, maybe not," Bonnie replied. "They *did* seem like nice people, and they really do like it here in Belle."

"I know it's a long shot, but any interest is better than no interest at all," Kit assured her friend. "A retired couple from out of state would surely need your help and Sara's and George's to keep the place running smoothly, too."

"My thought exactly," Bonnie agreed, then glanced at her watch. "Yikes, I'd better get going or I'll be late picking up Allison at the sitter's. Although that reminds me…" Bonnie lifted an eyebrow inquiringly. "How's it going with Simon?"

"Just fine." Kit offered her friend a bright smile. "He and Nathan are getting along just fine."

"How about you, Kit? Are you getting along with Simon just fine, too?" Bonnie prodded with a worried look.

"I don't know that I can do anything else but get along with him just fine," Kit admitted, her smile fading as she turned away. "Simon is Nathan's father. He loves Nathan and he wants to raise him as he has a right to do."

"But he's not going to cut you out of Nathan's life completely, is he? You're Nathan's guardian. Surely that entitles you to visitation, at the very least, and that shouldn't be hard to work out. You'll both be living in the Seattle area again by summer's end, won't you?"

"I'm sure we'll be able to work something out, one way or another, when the time comes," Kit assured her friend. Then she added in a tone she hoped wasn't too dismissive, "See you tomorrow, Bonnie? You, too, Sara?"

"Bright and early," they replied in unison, then laughed as they headed for the diner's front door.

Alone in the quiet diner, Kit turned out the lights, then crossed to the front door to lock it. She had given Simon a key to the side door on Monday—another relinquishment she hadn't appreciated having to make. She'd had no justification for restricting his freedom to come and go with his son as he pleased, though. He had rights she couldn't deny, especially if she hoped to stay on good terms with him.

Kit hadn't really allowed herself to think much about what kind of arrangements she and Simon might make so that she could continue to be a part of Nathan's life. That would have meant facing too fully the reality that all too soon he, not she, would be the little boy's primary caregiver—a reality she had wanted to avoid as long as possible.

But Bonnie had brought up a good point—one Kit had been too distracted to consider until now. She and Simon would both be living in Seattle by summer's end. That would put them into close enough proximity to make it easy for her to spend time with Nathan. And Simon.

Simon would have to want to allow it, though. As things stood between them now, however, including her in either of their lives, even in the smallest way, was probably the last thing he'd be inclined to do.

All her fault, Kit reminded herself again as she surveyed the kitchen one last time. And she was the only one who could remedy the situation. Maybe she should walk down to the park and attempt to make a friendly overture. Maybe by extending an olive branch of sorts, she could wheedle her way back into Simon's good graces.

Only, she was so totally wiped out that climbing the staircase to the apartment suddenly seemed almost more than she could do. She hadn't slept well for over a week, but she thought that if she could just make it up to her room now, and crawl into her bed, she'd be able to nap for the hour or so until Simon returned with Nathan. Then she wouldn't be quite so apt to snap if wheedling her way into Simon's good graces didn't work in her favor, after all.

Kit was halfway up the staircase when she heard the

telephone in the apartment ringing. Simon, she thought first, a clutch of fear deep in her heart—Simon calling to tell her that something had happened to Nathan. Or maybe to say he'd decided to take Nathan home to stay at the Double Bar S.

But he couldn't do that to her, could he? He wouldn't.

In her haste to answer the telephone, Kit not only quickened her pace, but also failed to watch where she was going. She forgot about the loose board near the top of the staircase—a board she had been intending to nail down for the past month. Only, it wasn't that bad, and if she remembered it was there and put her foot down exactly in the center rather than to one side—

One minute she was pounding up the stairs. The next minute the rubber sole of her sneaker caught on the loose board, throwing her off balance. She tried to stop herself from falling by grabbing at the banister, but her momentum was too great. She twisted around so that she was partially facing down the stairs instead of up, then landed on her bottom with a resounding thud, wrenching her left ankle in the process.

She cried out as much in surprise as pain. She couldn't believe she'd been so careless or so clumsy. Upstairs the telephone had stopped ringing, then started again, but she didn't try to get up again immediately. She took several deep breaths, trying to slow her pounding heart, not to mention calm down enough to assess whether she'd done herself any serious damage.

Thanks to her grip on the banister, she hadn't fallen hard enough to hurt her back. But when she stood and tried gingerly to put her weight on her left ankle, a sharp pain shot though the joint bringing tears to her eyes. As she sat again, the pain eased to a slightly more bearable degree, but still throbbed steadily.

"Okay, now what?" she muttered to herself, then to the telephone that had started ringing yet again, "Oh, shut up."

Whoever it was and whatever they wanted, she wasn't going to be of much help sitting on the staircase, her left ankle already beginning to swell. She should put some ice on it, then elevate it. But that meant going up to the apartment or down again to the diner. Either direction she chose, she'd have to scoot on her bottom.

Down would be easier than up, Kit decided after a few moments. Gravity would be on her side that way. Then she could hop from staircase to table, from table to table to the counter and from the counter to the kitchen on one foot. But not just yet, she thought, the tears in her eyes suddenly spilling over in annoyance, frustration and worst of all, shame.

Elbows braced on her knees, she put her head in her hands as tears trickled down her cheeks. She needed a few minutes to collect herself—not because twisting her ankle was any big deal. But a twisted ankle on top of everything else that had happened the past week qualified as a last straw. Under the circumstances, the desire to indulge in a good cry was certainly understandable, and hopefully would also be highly therapeutic.

That was how Simon found her fifteen minutes later when he came in through the side door of the diner, Nathan holding his hand and walking along beside him. Kit heard his key in the lock in time to dig a tissue from the pocket of her jeans, wipe her face with it and blow her nose. But she didn't even try to stand up to greet him.

"Kit," Nathan squealed, pointing to her as Simon halted

at the foot of the staircase. "Dahee…Kit?" Then, pointing to his feet as he had done regularly since Tuesday, he said, "See…boos…see boos, Kit?"

"Yes, sweetie, I see your boots," she said, her voice sounding just a little slurred from all the weeping she'd done.

"Are you okay?" Simon asked, starting slowly up the stairs with Nathan, his concern for her more than evident in the gentleness of his tone.

"Actually, I'm not," Kit admitted, unable to make even a small attempt at hiding her distress. "I tripped on a loose board I should have fixed weeks ago, and I fell and twisted my ankle and it's all swollen and I can't stand on it now."

She ended her tale of woe with a hiccup, then giggled, then unaccountably began to cry again. Help had arrived. There was no reason for more tears. Only she wasn't crying just because she'd hurt her ankle.

"Dahee…*Dahee,* Kit cwying," Nathan said, his voice sounding a little wobbly and very worried.

"I know, buddy. She fell down and went boom. But we're here now. We'll make it all better for her."

"Fall down, go boom?" Standing on the step just below her, Nathan patted her bent head with one small hand. "All better, Kit, all better?"

"Yes, I'm going to be all better now," she replied, gathering herself enough to offer the little boy a reassuring smile. To Simon she added, "Give me a hand up to the apartment. I want to put some ice on my ankle—"

"I think it would be better if I took you to the hospital emergency room." Kneeling down in front of her, he cradled her foot in one hand and ever so gently slipped off her sneaker with the other. The stroke of his fingertips against the swelling was incredibly soothing "You need to have this X-rayed."

"I'm sure it's just a sprain," she insisted.

"Probably so," Simon agreed. "But we're going to make sure it's not more serious than that. The way it's swelling up, I don't want to take any chances. Let me put Nathan in his car seat and pull the SUV closer to the side door. Then I'll come back for you, okay? It should only take me a few minutes."

"Okay."

"Promise to stay put until I can help you down the staircase?"

"I promise."

He started to turn away, then paused a moment and lifted Nathan into his arms. The look in his eyes as he met her gaze seemed almost to be one of relief.

"What?" she asked.

His scrutiny made her feel oddly uncomfortable.

"I was really worried about you," Simon said. "I tried calling you a few times to see if you wanted to meet us at the park, then maybe take a ride out to the ranch for dinner tonight. I was sure you'd said you weren't going anywhere after you closed the diner for the day, but then, you didn't answer…"

"I was on my way up the stairs when I heard the telephone ringing. I was in such a rush to answer it that I didn't watch where I was going. That's when I tripped and fell," she admitted sheepishly.

"Sorry about that." He offered her a shamefaced smile.

"My fault. I've had more than enough time to fix that loose board."

"I'm just as much to blame. I'd noticed it, too, but every time I thought about nailing it down, I got sidetracked. I'll take care of it as soon as we get back from the hospital."

"But it's my responsibility," Kit protested, then caught herself and blushed, aware of how ungrateful she must sound when that wasn't how she felt at all. "I'm sorry. What I meant to say, and should have been saying all along, is thank you very much."

"You're welcome." The corners of Simon's eyes crinkled as he favored her with another soft smile. "Now stay put until I can give you a hand."

"Yes, sir. Anything you say, sir," she replied, saluting him smartly.

"Anything?"

Simon's smile broadened into a wolfish grin and his bright eyes sparkled mischievously, causing her to blush even more deeply.

"Well, no…not *anything*…."

For the first time in days, Simon laughed out loud, making Kit realize how much she'd missed…*him*.

"I'll be right back," he said, turning away again.

"And I'll be right here."

In the time it took Simon to secure Nathan in the SUV and return to the diner to get her, Kit rode a roller coaster of high, then low, emotions. Relief at having Simon come to her rescue was quickly replaced by embarrassment at being caught by him in one of her clumsier moments.

But he had been so kind, so sweet and funny that just as swiftly she found herself smiling tenderly. And when she thought of the reason for the telephone call she'd been rushing to answer—*his* reason for calling her, the invitation he'd intended to offer—happiness bloomed anew deep in her heart.

Simon had intended to offer another chance for them to be friends instead of enemies—despite the antagonism she had shown him at every turn. She knew that she didn't deserve such consideration from him. But she was grateful for it, and she planned to let him know it.

"Okay, the boy is safe in his car seat, although none too happy about being left alone," Simon advised as he came through the side door of the diner again and moved briskly up the staircase.

"I think I can hop down the stairs and out the door if you'll just give me a hand." Grabbing ahold of the banister, Kit pulled herself up, careful not to put any weight on her injured ankle.

"How about if we play it safe and you just let me sweep you off your feet?" Simon asked with a teasing grin.

Before she could voice an indignant protest, he lifted her into his arms with amazing ease.

"I'm not sure such a drastic measure is absolutely necessary," she said a little breathlessly, not daring to look up at him as he walked down the staircase, holding her close.

The warmth of his muscular body penetrated the thin fabric of her T-shirt, making her all too aware of his masculinity. The spicy scent of his aftershave blended with the kiss of hot sun and fresh mountain air on his skin to tantalize her senses. And the steady beat of his heart so near the place where her cheek rested securely against his chest made her own pulse quicken with inexplicable anticipation.

She had injured her ankle. He was helping her out to his SUV the fastest and easiest way possible. *Sensual* as it might be to have him hold her in his arms, she would do well to remember that his intentions were anything but *sexual*.

"Maybe not absolutely necessary, but any excuse to get this close to you is a good excuse to me," Simon said.

His tone was light and laced with humor. But when Kit risked a startled glance at him, the gaze he directed her way was very serious and very, very steady.

"So you're saying that my sprained ankle is a good thing?" she asked, attempting to inject an equally teasing tone into her voice though she quickly looked away.

"Not at all, Miss Kit," he answered. "The good thing here, at least for me, is holding you close."

Again she couldn't think of a response fast enough. He had her out the side door of the diner and into the front passenger seat of the SUV while she was still trying to make sense of what he'd said.

Surely he had only meant to lighten the mood between them. He couldn't be interested in her in a physically intimate way, could he? Although the way he'd kissed her at the ranch...

Before Kit could follow the strange trail her thoughts had begun to take, Nathan's fussing from the back seat had her turning around to comfort him.

"It's all right, sweetie. I'm here now. We're going for a little ride with your daddy, okay?"

"'Kay..." Nathan replied in a quivery voice. Then, as he had only a few minutes earlier, he pointed to his new boots and smiled. "See boos, Kit. See Nafan's boos?"

"Yes, I do see your boots, big boy."

"Do you need anything from the diner before I lock up?" Simon asked.

"My wallet—that's where I keep my health insurance card," Kit said. "It's on the dresser in my bedroom."

"I'll get it for you and be right back."

* * *

The small regional hospital that served Belle and several other towns in northwestern Montana was a relatively short drive away. Traffic was also fairly light that late in the day on the normally busy two-lane highway. Most tourists heading for the park had already arrived by midafternoon, eager to check into the lodges and motels in the area as soon as they possibly could.

The hospital's emergency room was empty, as well, so they didn't have to wait too long to see the doctor on duty. Some thoughtful soul had put together a toddler-friendly toy box full of building blocks, cars and trucks, soft baby dolls and picture books that also helped to keep Nathan quietly occupied.

Kit's ankle was X-rayed, and after viewing the films and doing a bit of poking and prodding, the young doctor diagnosed a bad sprain. He fit her with an air cast—a lightweight contraption that braced her ankle better than an Ace bandage but still allowed her to wear her sneaker.

The doctor also advised her to keep her leg elevated as much as possible for the next two or three days, and otherwise to use the crutches also provided. She could gradually begin to put her weight on her injured ankle after a minimum of forty-eight hours. The air cast would provide the necessary support so that the risk of further damage would be minimal. She would probably be able to give up the air cast altogether within ten days, he predicted. By then, her ankle should be strong enough that she'd be able to walk without it, though still with a slight limp.

Kit listened to the doctor's instructions with increasing concern. Not due so much to the nature of her injury, but because of how it was going to affect her ability to work in the diner, and even more importantly, to care for Nathan. She could sit on a stool and work the cash register in the diner. But how was she going to be able to manage on her own with Nathan in the evenings?

Trying to keep up with the busy little boy while on crutches would be a real challenge. And how would she be able to get him in and out of his high chair or, for that matter, his bed? She wouldn't be able to pick him up while balancing on one leg or hanging on to a pair of crutches.

"Hey, it's not that bad," Simon said softly when the doctor left them alone in the examination room for a few minutes while he went to write a prescription for pain medication.

"I know," Kit conceded, trying to smile with only minimal success. "I could have broken a bone and ended up on crutches for several weeks instead of only a couple of days."

Back in the SUV, with Nathan beginning to fuss in earnest, Kit considered all that lay ahead of her once she was home again and couldn't help but feel overwhelmed. The practice runs she'd been forced to make on the crutches before she'd been allowed to leave the emergency room had done nothing for her overall confidence in coping on her own. She could all too easily fall and really hurt herself. How would she be able to take care of Nathan if she knocked herself unconscious?

"You know, I've been thinking," she began, then hesitated, twisting her hands together in her lap.

Kit hated what she was about to propose to Simon, but she knew that for Nathan's sake she had no choice.

"Yes, I gathered you were," Simon replied, glancing at her with a light but encouraging smile. "But I have an idea that whatever you've been thinking, it hasn't been especially good, has it?"

"I'm just really worried about how I'm going to be able to look after Nathan while I'm hopping around on crutches. I've realized that it would probably be a lot better for him—a lot *safer* for him, actually—if you…if you took him home with you to the ranch tonight," she said, expelling the last few words in a rush, giving herself no chance to change her mind.

Nathan's well-being was more important to her than anything else, and he would be going home for good with Simon soon enough anyway. By using her sprained ankle as a reason to take the first step in giving up her custody over the little boy, at least she'd have some small measure of control over the situation. Simon wouldn't be taking Nathan from her. Instead, she would be allowing Nathan to go with him of her own volition.

"What about you?" Simon asked, his glance now edged with surprise.

"Oh, I'll be fine…just fine," Kit assured him. "There's no need for you to worry—"

"I meant, what about you coming to stay with us at the ranch, too?" Simon cut in, sounding somewhat exasperated.

"I couldn't do that," Kit answered quickly, refusing to allow herself to be tempted by his invitation.

She couldn't—*wouldn't*—just show up at the Double Bar S on crutches, expecting Mitchell and Deanna Gilmore to take care of her. She was perfectly able to take care of herself. Nathan was the one who needed looking after, not her.

"Why not?" Simon asked, obviously unwilling to take her at her word.

"I have to run the diner, which I can do just fine even

hobbling around on crutches. I could probably manage all right with Nathan, too, but I'd rather not take the chance. If I lost my balance…" She shrugged and looked away. "He really will be safer with you at the ranch."

"But you'll be safer if we stay here with you," Simon pointed out patiently as he pulled to the curb in front of the diner. "That way I can keep an eye on both of you, and make sure neither one of you gets into any mischief."

"Oh, no, I couldn't ask you to do that," Kit said, unable to hide her alarm.

Though why she was so bothered by the idea of Simon staying with her in the apartment she couldn't really say. It wasn't as if she expected him to make a pass at her or anything. Only there had been that kiss at the ranch, and then the way he'd held her as he'd carried her down the staircase. But if he did come on to her, she could just say no…even if she really wanted to say—

"You didn't ask, Kit. I offered," Simon said as he switched off the engine. Turning in his seat, he gazed at her steadily, challenge glinting in his bright blue eyes. "Either I stay here with you and Nathan or the two of you come back to the ranch with me. One way or the other, it's your choice. But that's the only choice I'm giving you."

"Then I'd just as soon we stay here," she replied, relenting none too graciously. "It will be easier—at least for me."

"For me, too, actually," Simon said, opening his door. "Otherwise I'd have to bring you back to the Dinner Belle by seven in the morning to open up for the day. Staying here, at least I'll be able to get a little extra sleep." He waggled his eyebrows at her and grinned.

"But you don't have a change of clothes…"

"I always keep an overnight bag packed and stowed in the SUV."

"That's convenient," she muttered, unable to hide her consternation at what that seemed to imply.

"It has been—especially when I have to follow a story out of town on short notice," he told her. Then he added solicitously, "Need any help with those crutches?"

"I can manage."

"I'll get Nathan then."

Though he'd fussed for a while, the little boy had eventually fallen asleep on the drive home from the hospital. Kit knew there would be hell to pay later, but she saw no sense in warning Simon that they were going to be in for a long night. He'd find out soon enough how even one small glitch in Nathan's routine could make for a very cranky and—in the case of a late nap—a very wide-awake little boy about the time *they* would be more than ready to call it a night themselves.

"He's sleeping so soundly I hate to wake him up," Simon said as he worked at the straps on the car seat.

"Better now than any later," Kit advised.

"Why is that?"

"The longer he naps now, the longer he's going to want to stay awake past his usual bedtime, not to mention ours."

"I hadn't thought about that," Simon admitted.

"Just one of the joys of parenthood."

"Do you have to make that sound so ominous?"

"Ask me that question again at midnight," she advised him with a knowing smile.

A moment later, Nathan ended any hope of further conversation with a squall of two-year-old vexation, proving her point in spades.

Chapter Twelve

By the time Nathan finally fell asleep just short of midnight, exactly as Kit had predicted, Simon wanted nothing more than to crawl into the bed in the spare bedroom *alone*. He couldn't remember ever being quite as exhausted as he was at the end of that evening. He had trailed after Nathan, doing everything and anything he could think of, first to keep his son entertained, and then to get him into bed.

No longer on his normal daily schedule, the little boy had howled until Simon and Kit had put together a meal of diner leftovers. Instead of eating the baked chicken, noodles and sliced carrots, he had smeared his food all over the tray of the high chair, on his face and even in his hair.

He had howled again while Simon attempted to give him a bath, but had recovered his normally good humor enough to run around the apartment screeching and giggling in his pajamas until Simon tried to tuck him into bed.

Then he had howled yet again, not to mention each time thereafter that Simon took him back to the bedroom after a short respite.

Simon had insisted that he could look after his son on his own after they'd finished dinner. He'd urged Kit—suddenly much too pale and much too quiet—to take one of the pain pills they'd picked up at the hospital pharmacy and make an early night of it. She hadn't even pretended to protest. She had flashed him a very weary, very grateful smile, made a quick stop in the bathroom to wash her face and hands, then hobbled off to her bed and firmly closed the door.

Simon had wondered how much rest she would actually be able to get with all of Nathan's screeching and howling. Then he decided that any reprieve from a wound-up and ready-to-go two-year-old child was better than none at all. He also acknowledged that she had either been hurting pretty badly or had been knocked out completely by the pain pill not to venture out of her room even once to check on how he was holding up on his own with Nathan.

As his head hit the pillow and he closed his eyes at last, Simon also wondered how Kit had managed all alone the past three months, not only running the diner, but also seeing to Nathan's every want and need. She hadn't chosen either job, yet she had calmly and competently taken charge without any complaints.

Not many young women would have sidelined their own aspirations, even temporarily, to shoulder such demanding responsibilities. But then, not one of the young women he had known had had such a tender heart or such a caring soul as Kit Davenport. Certainly not Lucy Kane,

and certainly not the few women he had dated occasionally during the three years he'd lived in Seattle.

Too bad he hadn't appreciated Kit's qualities a long
time ago. He could have saved himself a lot of anguish.
But all wasn't completely lost. He had been given a chance
to make things right for himself, and hopefully for Kit and
Nathan, too.

Staying with her in the apartment 24/7 for the next few
days would give him an excellent opportunity to move in
that direction—once he'd had some sleep, of course. Taking a last look at his watch before setting it on the nightstand he saw that it was nearly one in the morning. Surely
Nathan would sleep until at least eight o'clock…maybe
nine. That would work for Simon. A good eight hours of
sleep and he'd be more than ready to perform his fatherly
duties once again.

"Hey, sleepyhead, time to rise and shine."

Just on the edge of wakefulness, Simon groaned low in
his throat. He recognized the soft, lilting voice disturbing
his well-earned, much-needed sleep, though it wasn't a
voice he'd expected to hear while he was still in *his* bed.
Only he wasn't in his bed, either at the Double Bar S or in
his high-rise condo in Seattle.

He was in the narrow bed in the sparsely furnished spare
bedroom in Kit's mother's apartment over the Dinner Belle
Diner, he recalled with a jolt of adrenaline that had him
blinking open bleary eyes. And Kit was sitting right there
beside him, her slim hip, clad in worn jeans, just inches from
his own hip, naked under the light cotton blanket he had
crawled beneath only…five—*was it only five?*—hours ago.

Simon groaned again, started to shift from his belly to

his back, then thought better of it when he realized a certain part of his anatomy was on very obvious, not to mention very high, alert. Instead, he moved just enough so that he could see Kit's face in the pale morning light.

He noted rather grudgingly that she not only looked very fresh, but also very rested. Obviously any concern he'd had that Nathan had kept her up last night had been completely unnecessary.

"Okay, I'm awake," he muttered. "But why? It's only six o'clock and it doesn't sound like Nathan's up yet."

"He's still sleeping, too, but you're going to have to get him up in a few minutes. Otherwise he'll be off his schedule again today, and that wouldn't be a good idea." Her smile was almost sympathetic as she put her hand on his shoulder for a moment. "I just wanted to let you know that I'm going down to the diner now."

"Thanks a lot."

"You look really beat. Was he really awful last night?"

"You didn't hear him running around like a wild man, screeching and howling like a banshee?" Simon asked in disbelief.

"No, not at all. That pain pill really knocked me out."

"Lucky you," Simon growled, then smiled up at her despite his cranky mood. "I take it you're feeling better today?"

"My ankle is still really sore and my upper arms ache from using these darn crutches, but otherwise I'm fine. How about you?"

"Just a little tired."

"Hang in there," she advised in a kindly tone. "You'll be able to take a nap with Nathan after lunch."

"Already I can hardly wait."

"I have to go now. Promise not to fall asleep again?"

"Promise." He yawned hugely as Kit pushed off the edge of the bed and balanced carefully on her crutches. "Can you make it down the stairs on your own?"

"I certainly hope so."

"I could always sweep you off your feet again," he offered with a quick grin.

The prospect of having Kit's warm body in his arms again chased away the last bit of his weariness.

Kit didn't even hesitate as she clumped steadily, perhaps even a bit more speedily, to the bedroom doorway, obviously chased away, period, by the mere thought of being held by him again.

"No, thanks," she said without a backward glance. "I'll be just fine. You see to Nathan, okay?"

Listening to Kit make her resolute way to the apartment door, Simon wondered why she continued to be so damned standoffish toward him. She seemed to have a natural friendliness about her with everyone else—the diner's many patrons, the staff at the hospital, Bonnie, Sara and George, even his parents. But every time *he* made an amiable overture, she brushed him off. And though she occasionally relaxed enough to joke with him, she always seemed to withdraw just when he began to believe he was finally making some headway with her.

Maybe he was at fault for holding back. He hadn't wanted to push her into acknowledging the sparks that had flown between them when he'd kissed her at the ranch, though. He knew that she was as intimately aware of him as he was of her, and he had expected her to respond accordingly of her own free will. But she seemed determined to ignore the admittedly somewhat muted signals he kept trying to send her way.

Perhaps the time had come for him to tell her as frankly as he could exactly how he felt about being with her. Better yet, maybe he should stop worrying altogether about offending her sensibilities. Maybe he should just throw her over his shoulder, carry her off to bed and *show* her, once and for all, that he wanted *and* needed her in his life, not only as his friend, but also as his lover and his mate.

She could still tell him to get lost—he *was* capable of taking *no* for an answer. But at least he would have been honest with her, thus eliminating that possible regret.

Having gotten less sleep than usual, Nathan was a real terror again that morning. Nothing Simon did seemed to please the little boy. He pouted and fussed as he roamed from room to room, obviously looking for Kit. Finally Simon took the little boy down to the diner near lunchtime. Teary-eyed, he clung to Kit as if it had been days instead of only a few hours since he'd last seen her.

Simon wouldn't have minded a cuddle himself. Instead, he stoically went to the kitchen and collected the containers Kit had filled with salad, spaghetti and garlic bread for their lunch.

She didn't look nearly as good as she had at dawn, he noted. Dark shadows had gathered under her eyes and her mouth was drawn down in a grim line, signaling that she must surely be in pain even though she made no complaint when they were all upstairs again. In fact, she said very little at all and only picked at her food.

"You must have had a really busy morning," Simon ventured.

He stowed the leftovers in the refrigerator, then set about cleaning up the mess Nathan had made.

"We had two tour buses full of senior citizens show up

at almost the same time," Kit said. "They filled every table and all the stools at the counter. What a day for me to be pretty much out of commission." Her smile was exceedingly wan as she glanced at the kitchen clock, then reached for her crutches. "I'd better get back. Bonnie and Sara are going to need all the help I can give them even if it's only ringing up the cash register."

"Hey, why don't you stay up here and rest while Nathan naps?" Simon suggested. "He's half-asleep already."

He tipped his head toward his son, nodding off in his high chair, finally too tired to fuss.

"But I can't abandon Bonnie and Sara."

"Not to worry—I can help out downstairs while you and Nathan nap." Simon released the little boy from his high chair, lifted him into his arms and retrieved his bottle from the warmer. "I may not have much experience waiting tables, but I'm a quick study and I have two good legs. With a little guidance from Bonnie and Sara, I shouldn't have trouble carrying plates to tables and cleaning up after the customers finish eating."

"You'd be a lot more help to them than I would," Kit admitted in a wry tone. "But I promised you a nap this afternoon, and you deserve one after putting up with Nathan's antics last night and again this morning."

"I admit that I had a hard time waking up this morning, but I'm fine now," he assured her. "I also have a confession to make. I've always thought it would be kind of fun to work in the diner."

"Really?" Kit eyed him with amusement as well as disbelief.

"Yes, really."

"Well, in that case, you're more than welcome to take

my place this afternoon," she said with a smile. "Might as well live the adventure while you have a chance, right?"

"Right." He smiled, too. "I'll get Nathan settled in his bed, then I'll head downstairs."

"And I'll just gimp into my room and snooze a while." Kit's smile now held a full measure of gratitude. "Thanks, Simon. I really appreciate all you've done. You really are a nice guy."

"Yes, I know." He gazed at her thoughtfully, then added, "I've been wondering when you'd realize it, too."

"I've always known you're a nice guy," she protested, a tinge of red staining her face.

"Couldn't prove it by me lately. But hey, it's not really that big a deal, is it?"

"I think it is to me, especially since I seem to have given you the impression that I don't think much of you. That's not true at all, Simon. I think a lot of you, quite a lot actually."

The steady way she looked at him served to emphasize the sincerity he heard in her voice, and hope sang anew in his heart.

"Again, I'm glad, because I think quite a lot of you, too," he said. "I also happen to think *about* you quite a lot, but that's another story altogether—one better left to another time. You need to rest a while and I need to get down to the diner and live my fantasy—at least one of them." He winked at her, then added, "I'll check on Nathan in a couple of hours or so, okay? And if you need me, just give a holler."

She eyed him for a long moment, her consternation obvious. He'd most certainly piqued her curiosity. But like him, she knew further discussion would have to be postponed.

"Have a good time," she said at last, her smile wry.

"I am already…the time of my life."

Touching a hand to her cheek, he smiled, too. Then he turned and walked out of the kitchen, Nathan in his arms, and a whole new world of possibilities awaiting him.

"So, was the diner experience everything you hoped it would be?" Kit asked that evening as Simon collapsed beside her on the living room sofa after tucking Nathan into bed.

Back to his normal routine and rested after his nap, the little boy had been in a much better mood the remainder of the day. Kit, too, had seemed to be feeling better after sleeping most of the afternoon. And while Simon was tired, it was the good kind of tired that comes from a job—actually several different jobs—well done.

"I have to admit it was a lot more work than I'd anticipated, but there were some rewards. Bonnie and Sara insisted on sharing their tips with me. I earned…" He paused and dug out a wad of money from the back pocket of his jeans. "Twelve dollars and some odd cents." He smiled proudly. "I'm happy to say that I didn't break a single plate or slide a single sandwich into anybody's lap, either."

"Good for you." Kit reached over and gave his arm a congratulatory squeeze.

"I have to admit, too, that I have a whole hell of a lot more admiration for everybody in the food-service industry. Keeping the customers happy isn't all that easy sometimes."

"Did you have to deal with a lot of complainers?" Kit's smile turned sympathetic.

"Not really, but I did get a lot of teasing from some of the locals," he said. "It was all Bonnie's fault, too. She insisted that I had to wear an apron if I wanted to wait on tables. Is that some kind of state law or something?"

"No, just Bonnie giving you a hard time," Kit replied with a chuckle. "Aprons aren't mandatory, but I bet you looked too cute wearing one."

"Oh, yeah, *too* cute. Winifred Averill laughed herself silly when she saw me rigged out in white eyelet." He shot a glowering look Kit's way. "At least I'll know better next time."

"I'll be able to work in the diner tomorrow," Kit said. "I feel much better after resting all afternoon, and my ankle is hardly swollen at all anymore." She wriggled her left foot now propped on a pillow on the coffee table. She had taken off the air cast because she was more comfortable without it when she had her leg elevated. "One more day on crutches, then I should be able to start walking without them, too."

"Don't rush it," Simon advised.

"I won't, but I do want to be able to get around on my own as soon as possible. I really hate being so dependent…"

"Especially on me?" Simon finished for her, shooting her a questioning glance as her voice trailed away.

"On anyone," Kit insisted. "It's nothing personal. I'm just so used to taking care of myself—to being independent."

"So you don't have a significant other back in Seattle with whom you've gotten used to sharing life's burdens?" Simon asked, his tone light, teasing her just a little.

He had spent most of the afternoon trying to come up with a way to get her to talk to him—really talk to him—about the past, the present and most important of all, the future he hoped they would have together. Now that she'd unwittingly given him an opening, he meant to take full advantage of it. The worst she could do was to tell him to mind his own business.

"I've had relationships—two, actually. Neither one was serious enough for happily ever after," Kit replied in a matter-of-fact tone. "The man I was seeing when my mother became ill had been offered a job in Atlanta. There was no way I could have gone with him, although he did ask me to. There was also no way he would have given up the chance to further his career to live with me here in Belle. We kept in touch for a while, but then Lucy died, and I became Nathan's guardian. Brent didn't really want a ready-made family, so we decided it was best to go our separate ways."

"I'm sorry," Simon said.

Not because Kit was no longer involved with Brent. She was much better off without a man who couldn't, or wouldn't, stand by her during hard times. The sympathy he felt for her was based solely on the fact that she'd been hurt by someone she'd loved and trusted.

"I'm not—not really." Kit gave a negligent shrug of her shoulders. "In fact I'm lucky that Brent showed his true colors before I got any more involved with him, emotionally, than I already was. Don't get me wrong—he's not a bad person. His priorities are just different than mine." She hesitated a moment, her gaze distant, then glanced at him with a considering look. "What about you, Simon? Do you have a significant other waiting for you and Nathan back in Seattle?"

Simon noted her mention of Nathan, pairing his son with him as a package deal, as indeed they would be from now on. Any significant other he had in the future would have to be willing and able to love his little boy. But the only *other* he wanted in his life now was Kit Davenport, and she already loved Nathan as if he were her own child.

He and Kit had been drawn together initially by their mutual love of his son. Maybe Nathan could also be the bond that kept them together until he managed to convince her of how important she was to *him*. Kit was free and so was he. To Simon's way of thinking, the first and highest hurdle had already been cleared.

"Like you, I've had a couple of relationships since I moved to Seattle, but neither one was serious enough to consider a walk down the matrimonial aisle. I was gun-shy for a long time after Lucy, and then I was traveling a lot for a while, following various stories for the paper. Of course, I won't be taking off for days at a time to destinations unknown anymore. That wouldn't be fair to Nathan."

"Will you be able to stay at the paper if you can't travel the way you used to?" Kit asked, a frown creasing her forehead.

"The editor of the Metro section will be retiring in a couple of months. A few days before my parents asked me to come home, the managing editor approached me about taking the job of associate editor when the current associate editor is promoted. I'd originally told him that I'd think about it. As soon as I found out about Nathan, though, I sent him an e-mail letting him know I'd take the job."

"So you'll be staying in Seattle at least for a while."

Kit glanced at him, then quickly away, but not before Simon saw the relief in her pale eyes.

"And you'll be there, too, finishing your graduate work at the University of Washington, right?"

"Right." She looked at him again, and this time her expression was slightly bemused. "Funny, isn't it, that we've both lived in the same city for the past three years but we've never run into each other?"

"I'm assuming you live out by the university?"

"Yes."

"I live downtown in a high-rise condo, so that could explain it—same city, but miles apart. I was also out of town a lot. Of course, you could have looked me up," he reminded her with a gentle nudge, shoulder to shoulder. "You knew I worked at the *Post,* didn't you?"

"Yes, but after what you did to Lucy, or rather, what I *thought* you did to her, you weren't exactly on my list of favorite people." She quirked an eyebrow and she nudged him back, then added, "You knew I was living in Seattle, too, didn't you? But you never bothered to get in touch with me, either."

"For much the same reason that you didn't contact me. You were Lucy's best friend, and Lucy broke my heart. Seeing you would have brought back memories of a time in my life that I just wanted to forget," Simon admitted. "Though I'm really sorry now that I didn't look you up."

"You would have known about Nathan a lot sooner," Kit said.

"I would have also had a chance to get to know you better a lot sooner, too," Simon reminded her.

Reaching over, he took her hand in his. To his relief, she didn't pull away. Instead, she turned her palm up and twined her fingers with his.

"I doubt I would have been any friendlier toward you than I was when you showed up in the Dinner Belle a week ago."

"But you would have found out that I wasn't the rounder you thought I was before the habit of hating my guts became so ingrained," he said, only half-teasingly.

"I never hated your guts, Simon," Kit retorted, a shade indignantly. "I was just very…disappointed with you."

"What about now? Am I still a disappointment to you?"

"Of course not. Now that I know Lucy lied to you, as well as to me, I understand why you stayed away from her."

"Did she ever come to Seattle to visit you?" he asked, partly out of curiosity, and partly to see if one of his theories about why Lucy had lied to him was correct.

"Not once. I invited her several times, too. She could have even come on her own. My mother offered to watch Nathan for her. She always had some excuse, though. I had begun to think that maybe she was afraid to get too far away from Belle. But that was hard to believe because Lucy never seemed to be afraid of anything. Still, it makes more sense now that I know she lied to you about Nathan so you'd go to Seattle without her."

"I didn't have to take the job at the *Post*," Simon said. "I could have stayed here and worked for my father."

"But it wasn't what you wanted to do."

"I would have anyway…then."

"But you would have hated it, and maybe her, too, eventually," Kit pointed out pragmatically.

Simon knew that Kit was right. He had never intended to be a rancher. He'd had too many other places to go, too many other things to do, and thankfully, his parents had understood. That was why his father had hired a business manager as well as a foreman to handle the day-to-day running of the Double Bar S when he was ready to retire.

Simon would have been miserable if he'd stayed in Belle, Montana, three years ago. As miserable, he now suspected, as Lucy would have been in a big city like Seattle.

"We were mismatched from the very beginning," Simon said, speaking his thoughts aloud.

"Not at the very beginning." Kit gave his hand a reassuring squeeze. "You just wanted to have fun together when you started dating, and you did. But then you each started wanting something different, and Lucy got pregnant, and I'm guessing, scared of what you would have expected her to do if you thought the baby was yours."

"She had to know I'd find out about Nathan eventually, though—especially if she stayed in Belle."

"I'm sure she did, although she never talked about it."

"She named you as his guardian in her will, but she didn't mention me at all." Simon hesitated a moment as the hurt Lucy had once caused him twisted his gut once again. "Like you said before, it's as if I'd given her some reason to cut me out of my own son's life. But I swear to you, Kit, I never did anything to give her cause to hate me that much."

"We'll never know why Lucy did half the crazy things she did." Gently Kit touched a hand to his cheek and turned his face until he reluctantly met her steady gaze, then added, "But I *know* she didn't hate you, and I also *know* she didn't have any reason to keep you from your son. I've seen you with him. It's obvious how much you love him. If I had been Lucy, I would have been so happy to be your wife and have your child—"

Kit stopped talking all at once and ducked her head in obvious confusion. As if, a heartbeat too late, she'd realized just how honest she'd finally been with him.

"But I'm not Lucy," she added primly. "I never was and I never will be."

"For which I'm eternally grateful," Simon said gently, refusing to let go of her hand when she tried to pull away. "I like you just the way you are, Kit Davenport. But you're making it damned hard for me to convince you of it with that brick wall you've built up against me."

"I haven't built up a brick wall against you," she protested.

"Oh, yes, you have," he said sternly, then added in the moment before he bent his head to claim a kiss, "But I'm about to start dismantling it…brick…by brick…by brick…."

Chapter Thirteen

I like you just the way you are, Kit Davenport...

Simon's statement, made in his quiet voice, rang with undeniable honesty as it echoed in Kit's mind. His kiss, tentative at first, then deeply insistent and darkly passionate after an endearing moment's hesitation, literally took her breath away. He had surprised her yet again. Sighing softly, she gave herself up to him, relaxing in his embrace. The intimacy of his claim seemed so good to her, and so very, very right.

Kit couldn't count the number of times she had stood on the sidelines in the past, watching Simon and Lucy together, wishing *she* could be the one he wanted. No matter how she tried to rationalize his desire for her now, or temporize her own response, she could do nothing but give in to the need she had tried so long—too long—to ignore.

She couldn't change the past and she dared not invest

in hope for the future. But for once in her practical life she had every intention of living for the moment, the incredibly wonderful moment, and enjoying to the fullest Simon's oh-so-tender ministrations.

Angling her head just so, teasing and tempting his tongue with hers, Kit threaded the fingers of one hand through his lush, silky, dark curls with feminine insistence, taking as much as she gave. Following her cue, Simon shifted next to her, moving his hand from her waist slowly up her back, then around to cup her breast.

Though too many layers of clothing kept his bare palm from her naked skin, the weight and warmth of his touch sent a shaft of hot desire through her belly. She sighed again, arching against him, seeking more of the pleasure his much-too-clever fingers seemed to promise.

With a low moan, Simon quickly moved his hand away, lifted his head and broke off their kiss. Kit stared up at him in sudden confusion, afraid she had given the wrong signals, or worse, somehow made the even more horrid mistake of misreading *his* intentions.

He looked back at her, his own gaze oddly assessing and almost…dispassionate. Her desire cooled by a wave of unforeseen embarrassment, Kit turned away from him and primly clasped her hands in her lap.

"Well, that obviously wasn't a good idea," she muttered, much as she had after he'd kissed her at the ranch.

A hot flush seared her face, betraying the depth of her discomfort despite the levity with which she spoke.

"Actually, I thought it was an excellent idea," Simon said, his voice incredibly kind as he touched her cheek, then gently but insistently turned her face so that she was forced to meet his probing gaze. "But I want to do more than play bump and tickle with you on the living room sofa. I want to make love with you, Kit, but only if you want it, too. Otherwise I'd just as soon take myself off to bed alone…while I still can." He stroked a thumb along the line of her jaw, holding her gaze for another long, quiet moment, then asked with obvious reserve, "So tell me, Miss Kit, what do *you* want to do?"

"I want to make love with you, too, Simon," she answered, offering him a soft smile.

His expression eased, as well. The lines of tension and concern etched on his forehead and along the sides of his mouth disappeared as if by magic. But still he seemed to hesitate.

"I don't want to rush you," he said. "And I don't want you to have any regrets."

"You're not, and I won't," Kit assured him. "I'm a big girl, I'm stone-cold sober, and I'm capable of taking full responsibility for the choices I make. Although there is one thing…"

She cocked an eyebrow at him, dismayed by the possible predicament that had suddenly come to mind, her smile taking on a wry edge as her voice trailed away

"What would that be?" Simon prompted with sudden concern.

"I'm not on the Pill, and I don't have any condoms handy," she said. "So unless you're better prepared than I am, you'll have to take yourself off to bed alone after all."

"Not to worry, sweetheart." Simon's grin held a mixture of relief and satisfaction. "I have some in my overnight bag. Not that I've actually needed them anytime in the recent past, I hasten to add."

"So you believe in being prepared for any eventuality

when you have to follow a story out of town, huh?" she questioned only half-teasingly despite the little addendum he'd included.

"Would you have been disappointed if I hadn't been?" he asked right back, eyeing her steadily.

Kit didn't need even a moment to consider her response.

"I would have been very disappointed," she admitted, her smile suddenly turning shy.

She needed the closeness, the physical as well as the emotional intimacy Simon wanted to share with her that night. She had carried too many burdens alone for too long. Being with him would be a respite of sorts, one she refused to deny herself.

She didn't need promises of happily-ever-after he more than likely wasn't prepared to offer her. Nor did she need avowals of mad, passionate love and conjugal fidelity. Allowing Simon to make love to her tonight with the tenderness and affection he'd always shown her in the past would be enough to soothe her weary soul.

Simon, too, smiled again, also with the merest hint of constraint.

"Would it be out of order to carry you to your bedroom, ma'am?" he asked with just the right touch of deference.

"Not at all, sir. But I'd better bring along my air cast and crutches so I'll have them handy later."

"I'll come back for them, promise."

Simon stood and slipped his arms around her, lifted her easily off the sofa and carried her without noticeable effort into the room that had once been her mother's.

Kit had moved her things there after Dolores's death so that Lucy could have her old room all to herself. Now that room was empty. So many changes in such a short time, Kit thought with a fleeting sense of melancholy. Soon she would be packing up everything in the apartment one last time.

But as Simon set her on the bed she'd made only haphazardly that morning, and turned on the lamp on the nightstand, Kit refused to allow either past memories or future worries to linger in her mind. Tonight the longing that had lingered in her heart for so many years would finally be assuaged. Tonight she and Simon would be together at last, and tonight that was all that really mattered to her.

With a promise to check on Nathan, Simon returned to the living room to retrieve Kit's cast and crutches. In the time that he was gone, she undressed and slipped under the quilt. The sheets cool against her bare skin, she lay quietly waiting for him, the rapid beating of her heart causing her pulse to pound with anticipation.

She could have been coy, hiding her eagerness for the touch of his hands, his mouth. But her feelings for Simon were pure and honest, and certainly no cause for shame. She had kept her love for him a secret long enough, perhaps to her own detriment. Had she allowed her feelings for him to be known sooner, maybe she would have been the one he'd desired all those years ago.

Kit knew she had done the right thing when she saw the surprise and the delight in Simon's eyes as he joined in her in the bedroom once again. His lazy smile held more than a hint of masculine pride and the gleam in his bright blue eyes as he met her gaze held not only a hint of playfulness, but also an intensity of purpose.

Just looking at him, still fully clothed, Kit felt her body softening with desire, her mouth going dry with expectation.

"Is Nathan okay?" she asked, her voice low.

Simon set her cast and crutches within easy reach of her side of the bed. Then he crossed to the nightstand where he deposited the aforementioned box of condoms.

"He's sleeping soundly," he replied as he sat beside her on the bed. "How's your ankle doing?"

"A little twinge every now and then, but otherwise not too bad at all," she assured him.

"I'll be gentle," he promised, smoothing a hand over her hair.

"I know you will." She offered him a teasing smile. "But I'm hoping you'll be naked, too—like *real* soon."

Simon laughed with undisguised enjoyment.

"What?" Kit demanded.

Surely she hadn't been all that forward under the circumstances.

"You never cease to amaze me, Kit Davenport." He quickly dispensed with boots, socks, jeans, denim shirt and briefs, then added, "I keep thinking you're the shy, quiet little girl I used to know, when I should be remembering that you're really a stubborn, independent, headstrong woman who neither wants nor needs to be handled with kid gloves."

"Well, *finally*," she murmured as he slid under the quilt and gathered her close in his arms.

"Meaning?" he asked, nibbling on her neck, his warm, moist breath a tickle on her sensitive skin.

"Finally you've seen the real me, and finally…" She sighed softly and snuggled close to him, reveling in the hard feel of his muscular, masculine body against the curves of her femininity. "Finally…being here with you…like this…"

"It is good, isn't it?" he asked.

His hands touched her breasts, her belly, the insides of her thighs, and his lips tasted their tantalizing way down the side of her neck to the base of her throat.

"Oh, yes, Simon, it's very, very good," Kit breathed on a whisper of delight.

She was torn between wanting him to hurry, hurry, hurry—to satisfy the desire that had her arching against him feverishly, sighing, then moaning as her senses ignited, and the wish that the special moments they now shared together would never end.

Not to be rushed despite her urging, Simon took his sweet, sensual time with her. He kissed her long and slow and deep, then he playfully nipped at her neck. He plucked her nipples with clever fingers, then laved them with his moist, velvet tongue. He cupped her womanhood possessively in the palm of his hand, then pressed a knowing thumb here and delved with his fingers there, until she writhed under him, flushed and panting and pleading.

Still consummately in control, Simon rolled away from her for a long moment and sheathed himself protectively. Then he moved between her legs again, the evidence of his desire pulsing at her threshold. Looking down at her, he spoke her name softly, inflected with the merest question.

"Let me love you," he said, his gruff voice darkened by the depth of his desire.

"Yes," she murmured, her own voice a mere whisper as she threaded her fingers through his lush curls and urged him closer for a kiss. "Yes, Simon…yes, please…."

He entered her then with one swift, sure stroke, filling her aching emptiness. She lifted her hips and opened herself to him without the slightest hint of reserve.

"Oh, Kit, you feel so good to me…so damned good…."

"You, too, Simon…you feel so good to me, too," she said, arching to meet his thrusts, urging him deeper still.

"I don't think I can…hold back…any longer…." he gasped.

"Finally…"

Pleased with the power she now had over him, Kit laughed softly. The ripple of her good humor coursed through him as well as through her, making him catch his breath as he brought them both to completion with several deft, deep, deliciously devastating strokes.

They lay together afterward for several long, quiet moments. Their breathing slowed incrementally to a more normal rate, as did their pounding hearts. Their heated bodies began to cool, as well.

Kit wished that they could stay just as they were forever, bonded in the deepest, most physically intimate way possible. Making love with Simon had taken her to a new plateau where she had experienced for the first time the truly dizzying heights of passion ultimately fulfilled. All too soon, however, tangible thoughts began to creep, unbidden, into her muzzy mind, dispersing the hazy afterglow of the pleasure she'd enjoyed.

Yes, making love with Simon had been wonderful, Kit acknowledged. But she knew better than to attach any great significance to the physical release they'd shared. They were both young, healthy, reasonably attractive, heterosexual adults. Due to their past relationship, they weren't strangers, and because they each loved Nathan dearly, they now shared important common ground.

Thrown together as they had been for over a week, occasionally as friends, but also often as adversaries, it was understandable that their emotional awareness of each other would be heightened into the kind of sexual tension that demanded eventual release.

"You haven't fallen asleep, have you?" Simon asked, his husky voice laced more with laughter than concern.

"No, I'm just savoring the moment."

Kit gave him a tiny, biting kiss on the shoulder, then shifted against him as he rolled to his side.

"It was good between us, wasn't it?" he said, more in affirmation than as an honest question or a statement of disbelief. "Really good."

He smoothed a hand over her hair, then slid a finger under her chin, tilting her face so that she had no choice but to meet his steady gaze.

"Oh, yes, it was really good between us, Simon," she assured him without the slightest hesitation, noting how his eyes lit up with masculine vanity. "But now..." She couldn't help the yawn that escaped her as she snuggled against his chest again. "Sorry, it's not the company."

"Well, that's a relief." He hugged her close, then yawned, too, and laughed. "May I just say ditto?"

"Only if you're sure I'm not boring you," Kit teased.

"Not in the least, as I'll be more than happy to prove to you if you'll just give me a minute or two to get cleaned up." Easing away from her, he sat up, then tucked the quilt around her shoulders. "Can I give you a lift to the bathroom or get you something to drink?" he added with a quirk of an eyebrow, reminding her of her injured ankle.

"I'm fine right now, but maybe later."

Good as his word, Simon was gone only a few minutes, and sleepy as she was, Kit welcomed him back to her bed with a smile that also held more than a hint of invitation in it.

She realized that she hadn't taken the time to really look at him when he'd first undressed. She had been too eager to feel the touch of his hands and mouth upon her then. Somewhat sated now, she allowed her gaze to rove over him, visually taking in his masculine contours with unabashed pleasure. She also noted with feminine delight the evidence of his rekindled desire.

"The way you're looking at me, you remind me of a kid in a candy store," Simon commented as he slid into bed with her again.

"And that's a bad thing?" she asked with a mischievous smile.

"As I'm quite sure you noticed before I crawled under the bedcovers, a certain part of my anatomy doesn't think so," he replied. "But I know you're tired."

"Not so tired that I'd turn down another taste of you," she murmured. Kissing him on the cheek, then on his jaw, his shoulder…his chest…his belly…she scooted down the bed. "Only if you're up to it, though. You *did* have a busy day."

"Oh, baby, I'm *so* up…to…it…" he muttered.

As she moved lower still, making clever use of her lips, her teeth and her tongue along the way, he threaded his fingers through her hair and moaned low in his throat.

Smiling to herself, Kit reveled in her renewed sense of power over Simon. For this moment in time he was hers, and hers alone. Pushing all thought of the future from her mind, she focused only on loving him with tender care. Then, as he reached for her, pulled her up and rolled her over, she allowed herself to be loved by him, as well.

* * *

Kit slept after their second round of lovemaking as if she'd been drugged, any dreams she had too fleeting to remember. Having Simon's solid weight and warmth right there beside her seemed only natural, adding to the soul-soothing peace that enveloped her.

No matter what happened in the days to come, she'd thought in the moments before she'd drifted off to sleep, she would always hold the beauty of this night with him close in her heart. She had shared with him so much more than she'd ever dared to hope.

But she also knew that in the cold light of day they would both be forced to face reality once again. One night of hot sex did not guarantee a future together, and she had no intention of acting as if it did.

So sound asleep was she that she didn't realize Simon had gotten up the next morning until he gently roused her with the soft stroke of a hand on her hair and the subtle aroma of freshly brewed coffee wafting from the mug he'd brought for her. Opening bleary eyes, she saw at once that he wasn't only awake, but also showered, shaved and dressed. She thought she caught the scent of bacon in the air, as well, along with just a hint of his spicy aftershave.

Kit hadn't realized just how alluring one's sense of smell could be, especially so early in the morning. The peace she'd felt the night before deepened as she yawned delicately, stretched her arms above her head and wriggled her toes under the bedcovers.

"Mmm...this is nice," she said, smiling up at Simon.

"Waking up at six-fifteen after less than a full night's sleep?" he asked, returning her smile with the merest hint of a grin.

"Waking up to a handsome man *and* a mug of hot coffee," she replied.

Keeping the quilt tucked modestly around her shoulders, she struggled to sit up against the pillows he plumped for her after he set the mug on the nightstand.

She didn't add that it was also something she could get used to doing. It was one thing to behave wantonly in a man's arms during a night of unexpected passion. It was another thing altogether to put that same man in an emotionally unacceptable position the next morning.

There had been no talk of the future and certainly no promises made between them. While they hadn't exactly had *casual* sex, they weren't even close to having a *committed* relationship, either. Although there were some who might consider her a candidate for commitment after her crazy, wholly-out-of-character conduct with him.

"I hated having to get you up at all," Simon admitted, sitting beside her on the bed. "But it's almost time for me to get Nathan up. You wouldn't have gotten much rest after that, and I know you have to get down to the diner, too."

"Yes, that's true," she agreed, then took a first delicious sip of the coffee he'd made for her.

"I thought you might need a hand getting to the bathroom, too,"

"I'm sure I'll be able to manage okay."

"How's your ankle today?"

"Still a little sore, but otherwise it feels a lot better," she said. "I may try to go without the crutches today and just wear the air cast."

"There's no rush for you to do that, you know."

"Says the man with two good legs," she quipped.

"I just meant that I don't mind staying here with you," he said, brushing the knuckles of his hand against her cheek in an almost chiding manner.

"I don't mind having you here, either," Kit admitted. "But I would still like to be able to get around without those blasted crutches."

"So you're not going to kick me out as soon as you're hobbling around on your own again?" Simon asked, eyeing her quite seriously.

"Oh, no," Kit assured him with a bright smile. "I think it's really good for you to have the extra time with Nathan. You two have a lot of lost time to make up."

"And…?" He hesitated, still looking pensive, then added, "That's the only reason I'm welcome to stay here?"

"It's as good a reason as any, isn't it?" Still smiling brightly, she set her mug on the nightstand, then made a shooing motion with her hand before he could reply. "You'd better get Nathan out of bed," she advised, adding, "I need to get going myself. Otherwise I'll never make it down to the diner by seven o'clock."

Simon looked at her for a few silent moments longer. He seemed disappointed and Kit, too, suffered a pang of remorse. But she refused to allow herself to read into the past evening's events anything that even hinted at permanence.

Simon had said he *liked* her just as she was. But when he spoke of Lucy, he used the word *loved.* That alone was enough to guarantee she couldn't, wouldn't, bank on having any kind of future with him.

"I have bacon and scrambled eggs warming in the oven," he said at last, picking up her mug. "My cooking is probably not as good as George's, but I was hungry and thought you might be, too."

"Actually, I'm starving," she replied, glad that he chose not to press her any further. "I'm also of the belief that any meal cooked by anybody but me is a good meal. Give me fifteen minutes and I'll be ready."

"Use the crutches, okay?" he urged. "Just to be safe."

"Okay, just to be safe." She smiled at him and waggled her hand again. "Now go get Nathan out of bed. Otherwise there will be heck to pay later."

"We don't want that, do we? Especially with what *I* have planned for later."

Simon shot her a sexy grin that sliced straight through her heart. Then he strolled out of the bedroom without a backward glance.

Feeling just a tad weak in the knees, Kit tossed aside the quilt and reached for the robe only he could have left for her at the foot of the bed. She didn't dare contemplate too closely what, exactly, he had in mind for later. Just knowing, as she did, that it would be something she liked was enough to start her heart pounding all over again.

She had way too much to do before they could be alone together again to get into a tizzy. So Simon wanted to stretch their night of passion into another—that only meant he'd enjoyed her company. There was no reason they couldn't have a little more…fun together, either—no reason, at all.

And that was all it would be—another night of fun. Under the circumstances, that was all it could be.

But was that going to be enough?

Chapter Fourteen

By Friday, Kit was getting around without her crutches, though she was still wearing the air cast and still favoring her left ankle with a noticeable limp. There was no need for Simon to continue to stay with her and Nathan in the apartment above the Dinner Belle Diner. But she hadn't indicated in any way that she wanted him to leave, and he certainly wasn't about to offer on his own to go back to the ranch.

The past few days, and nights, living with Kit and Nathan as if they were a family had given Simon a taste of something he hadn't realized was missing from his life.

There was the physical intimacy with Kit, of course. His passion for her, now lying constantly just below the surface, always at the ready, flared at the slightest provocation, ignited by a certain smile, an inflection in her voice, the casual touch of hand to arm, the bump of hip to hip.

But it wasn't just their sexual coupling, or rather, their lovemaking, as he had come to think of their bedroom romps, that he needed. His feelings for her were anything but casual. Nor was she merely a passing fancy. He couldn't think of a better way to start the day than waking up with her in his arms.

Watching her tend to Nathan with gentle, loving care, he saw the goodness that was innately hers. He could talk to her about almost anything, whether esoteric or mundane. Together, too, they laughed often and their laughter made his spirits soar.

All should have been well in his world, Simon thought as he sat on the living room floor with Nathan on Friday afternoon, building, then toppling castles made out of wooden blocks. He and Kit seemed to be moving forward on the same path, their union strengthened by their love for Nathan as well as their increasingly auspicious feelings for each other. Yet he couldn't rid himself of the suspicion that he'd missed some important warning signal somewhere along the way.

Admittedly there had been a moment or two when Simon wondered if Kit had only gone to bed with him as a means of securing her position in Nathan's life. But her response to him that first night, and each night thereafter, had been too fervent, not to mention too uninhibited, to be faked in any way. Nor had she indicated by so much as a single word that she expected him to do anything but take over the responsibility for his son completely on his own in the very near future.

Kit seemed to be holding a part of herself at a distance, as if she didn't quite trust him. She also seemed determined not to explore the possibility that they could have a future together. Instead, she seemed to accept the fact they would inevitably part ways, and her acceptance, Simon suddenly realized, was what kept prompting him to feel as if he were waiting for the proverbial other shoe to drop.

He had all but taken it for granted that they were a couple when she'd allowed him to stay past the time when she'd needed his help 24/7. But he had grown less and less sure since then, not to mention less and less confident about broaching the subject with her.

Checking his watch, Simon saw that it was almost three-thirty. Usually Kit finished shutting down the diner by three-fifteen at the latest, and today she knew that he was waiting to take Nathan to the park until she could also go along with them.

Curious as to what was keeping her downstairs, he stood and dusted off the seat of his jeans. Nathan looked up at him expectantly, his building blocks forgotten.

"We go, Dahee?" the little boy asked. "Go play…park?"

"We have to get Kit first." He swung his son into his arms. "Okay, little buddy?"

"'Kay, Dahee…get Kit," Nathan replied, grinning agreeably.

As he walked down the staircase, Simon noticed that the lights were still on in the diner. Though he didn't see anyone sitting at any of the tables, he heard a voice he didn't immediately recognize coming from the kitchen. Kit hadn't mentioned that she was expecting any after-hours visitors that afternoon. But neither did it sound like she was having a staff meeting with Bonnie, Sara and George.

"…and, of course, all the appliances have been updated within the past three years, and they're all still under warranty," Kit said as Simon paused in the kitchen doorway.

"Everything seems to be in excellent shape here."

The man standing by the six-burner stove—part of a

couple who appeared to be in their early sixties—nodded approvingly as his gaze swept over the immaculately clean work areas. His wife also looked around with ill-concealed excitement as Cassie Holden, Mountain View Realtors' premier sales agent, smiled serenely.

This must be the couple from Texas Kit had casually mentioned might be interested in buying the Dinner Belle. To Simon, they seemed much more eager than Kit had let on. But then, she probably hadn't wanted to get her hopes up without good reason, though she appeared to have now.

He knew he should be happy for her—selling the diner was what she not only wanted, but also needed to do so that she could continue her graduate work in Seattle. Yet once she sold the Dinner Belle, she wouldn't have any reason to return to Belle, Montana…unless he gave her one.

"Hey, Simon, and Nathan, sweetie pie," Kit said.

The gladness in her voice assured Simon that she was happy to see them as she crossed to the kitchen doorway where he still stood.

"Hey, Kit…I didn't mean to interrupt."

"You're not interrupting at all. Did you guys get tired of waiting for me?"

Nathan crowed with delight when she tweaked him on the cheek, then reached out for her eagerly.

"I was beginning to wonder what was keeping you," Simon admitted as he shifted Nathan into her arms.

"Cassie stopped by with Mr. and Mrs. Eastman as I was getting ready to close the diner for the day," she explained, nuzzling Nathan's neck. "She was just about ready to show them the apartment, weren't you, Cassie?"

Kit glanced back at the real estate agent who nodded in agreement.

"Yes, indeed, the Eastmans are really anxious to see the apartment."

"Then we'll leave you to it," Kit said. "Just let me grab my purse and Nathan's diaper bag."

"I'll run upstairs for you," Simon offered, already turning to head for the staircase.

"What a darling little boy," Mrs. Eastman said. "You and your husband must be so proud of him."

"Oh, Simon's not my husband, and I'm not Nathan's mother. I've just been helping out with him," Kit replied.

Her blithe tone caused a tiny hitch of pain in Simon's heart as he started up the stairs.

Was she really as nonchalant about their relationship as she sounded?

Simon knew of only one way to find out, and that was by asking her. Only he wasn't sure he was ready to hear her answer. He didn't like thinking that she could slip away from him sometime in the near future without any remorse. *Knowing* that she could, *knowing* that she *would,* would be even worse, especially when he was also sure she'd still want to be a part of Nathan's life.

Simon couldn't imagine how he'd handle seeing Kit without also being able to hold her, kiss her and *claim* her as a man needed to claim the woman he loved. But he might have to do more than consider such an unfortunate situation as only a possibility. He might have to live it as a bitter reality unless he finally laid his heart on the line.

"Your son needs a bath." Kit lifted Nathan from his high chair after dinner Friday night and wrinkled her nose as she plopped a kiss atop his curly head. "A shampoo, too. Right, stinky boy?"

"Tinky boy, tinky boy," Nathan chortled with unabashed delight.

"I suppose I should do the honors since I'm the one who let him stomp around in the dust pile at the park," Simon said.

"You *did* think it was amusing," she reminded him as she handed over his giggling, squirming son.

"Well, he was having such a good time, and what's a little more dirt on a busy boy?"

Simon grinned at Kit with fatherly pride as he slung Nathan over his shoulder and gave him a good-natured pat on the bottom.

"Pour an extra measure of the baby bubble bath into the tub and don't forget the conditioner for his hair. We don't want tangles in his little curls, do we?"

"No, ma'am, we most certainly do not," Simon acknowledged. "Why don't you stretch out on the sofa, switch on the television and relax a while? I'll clean up the kitchen after I get Nathan ready for bed."

"That's a tempting offer, but there's not much to do in here besides toss out burger wrappers and French fry cartons."

"You forgot to add hosing down Nathan's high chair to the list," he reminded her with a grin. "How can one very well-supervised little boy make such a mess without really trying?"

"It's the red ketchup—he just loves smearing it all over everything. Maybe he's going to grow up to be a famous artist."

"We could only be so lucky," Simon tossed back as he headed down the hallway.

He was in the midst of rinsing the conditioner out of Nathan's hair while his son splashed water into the air, and also all over him, with the palms of his hands, when he heard the faint ring of Kit's telephone. She answered immediately, but the conversation must not have been especially long.

She was sitting on the sofa, channel-surfing with the remote control, when he joined her a few minutes later. Nathan, dressed in his pajamas, his hair still a little damp, ran to her as Simon followed after him, then crawled into her lap, ready for a last snuggle before bed.

"Cassie called," she said, looking up at him.

"I heard the telephone ring." He sat beside her, then eyed her questioningly. "Was it anything important?"

"She's pretty sure the Eastmans are going to make an offer on the diner. They especially liked the upstairs apartment. They won't have to buy a place to live along with the business itself."

Kit related the information in a matter-of-fact tone, her gaze on the television screen where the host of a biweekly news program introduced a segment on home-repair rip-off schemes. Unable to read any expression at all on her face, Simon wasn't quite sure how to respond.

"So…is that good?" he asked after hesitating a moment more.

Kit rubbed her cheek against Nathan's silky soft curls and gave a seemingly negligent shrug of her shoulders.

"Well, yes, actually it is," she replied. "They're the first ones to look at the diner who have shown any real interest in buying it. They also seem like nice people, and from what they said to me, it sounds like they're more than willing to keep George, Bonnie and Sara on the payroll."

"But?" Simon prodded, hearing the uncertainty in her voice.

"But they told Cassie that they would only buy the diner

with the understanding that I'll be out by mid-July at the latest. They want to have a few higher income months before the winter weather really sets in." Kit shrugged again, still without looking at him. "I thought I'd be able to stay until August, but if it's a matter of moving back to Seattle a little sooner than I'd planned to make the sale, then that's what I'll do."

"If you wanted to stay in Belle until the end of the summer, you'd be more than welcome at the ranch," Simon said, touching her arm, trying to get her to look at him.

"I appreciate the offer." She slid him only the slightest glance, then stood with sleepy-eyed Nathan still held close in her arms. "But once I've turned over the diner to the Eastmans, I might as well head back to Seattle. I'm going to have a lot to sort out there before my graduate classes begin in September." She hesitated a moment, rubbing her cheek against Nathan's curls again and gazing off into space. Then she seemed to give herself a mental shake before she added briskly, "Come help me put your son to bed?"

"'Kay," he said, mimicking Nathan's favorite form of response.

To his relief, Kit finally offered him a smile as she turned to lead the way to the little boy's bedroom.

They had done a good job of wearing Nathan out at the park. One arm slung around his teddy bear, he was asleep almost as soon as they'd tucked him into his bed.

Standing beside Kit, Simon could feel her begin to relax. He, too, sensed his own tension easing, as he looked down at his son, so peaceful and serene. No matter how many cares and concerns he had, he knew what mattered most to him—Nathan, of course, but Kit, too, in equal measure.

There were decisions looming for both of them, individually and together as a couple. He didn't want to influence her unduly, or pressure her one way or another. But he had to let her know how much he cared about her. He couldn't let her think that he considered her no more than a temporary diversion. He owed that not only to her, but also to himself.

There was a chance that Kit's feelings for him weren't as deep and true as his feelings for her. Much as he hated to face such a possibility, Simon knew better than to discount it altogether. She obviously loved his son, but that didn't mean she loved him, as well.

Her signals lately had most certainly been mixed, and he had never been good at reading between the lines. He didn't want to think that she'd prefer not to spend the rest of her life with him. But if that turned out to be the case, then he would be grateful for what they *could* have together—the bond of Nathan and the closeness of a very special friendship.

"When he's asleep it's hard to believe what a little wild man Nathan can sometimes be," Kit mused as she trailed a gentle fingertip across the little boy's forehead.

"He can be a real toot when he wants to be, can't he?" Simon agreed, unable to hide his masculine pride.

"Oh, yes, but he's come by it naturally."

Kit nudged him with an elbow and offered him a teasing smile.

"Are you saying I can be a wild man, too?" Simon asked, his voice soft.

Putting an arm around her shoulders, he drew Kit close for a long, slow, deep kiss.

"I've seen evidence of it, " she admitted a bit breathlessly when he finally let her go, long enough for her to answer.

"Would you like to see more of the same?"

"Well, I wouldn't want to put you to any trouble."

"Believe me when I say it's no trouble at all, sweetheart," he growled, nibbling at her neck.

"Say whatever you want, Simon Gilmore, but I'd much rather have you *show* me just what a toot *you* can be."

"Then you'd better come right this way, Miss Kit."

Taking her by the hand, Simon led her out of Nathan's bedroom, across the hallway and into her room without the slightest hesitation.

He wanted her so desperately he could have stripped them both of their clothing, slung her across the bed and claimed her without missing a beat. But such caveman tactics would have only satisfied him temporarily, and Kit likely not at all. He wanted to do better than that for her, and for himself, as well. He wanted to bring her to slow, excruciatingly sweet completion once. Then he wanted to do it all over again.

In fact, he did exactly that as the night spun away in a haze of pleasure. First he made love to her with only his mouth, and later, after she had managed to catch her breath, he made love to her again in a more traditional way, taking for himself, as well, a full measure of the most intense satisfaction he'd ever experienced in his life.

Sated but not yet asleep, Simon held Kit close in his arms as they came down slowly from the exquisite high of their lovemaking. She seemed as content as he did to lie quietly in the pale glow of moonlight shining through the curtains on the windows. Each beat of her heart was in sync with his, each inhalation she took matching the rhythm of his own measured breathing.

He thought of the phrase "And two became as one," and understood at last that it could really happen in the right place, at the right time, with the right person. But still he sensed a subtle tension in her, as well as in himself, that should have long since been dispelled.

Shifting slightly, he glanced at her and noted with a pang of trepidation the pensive look on her lovely face. Obviously all was not right with her world despite his every effort to make it so. As open, honest and joyous as her physical response to him had been, she now seemed consumed by the worries that had burrowed into her psyche over the past few months.

She had dealt with so many traumas on her own for so long. Only time and effort on his part would convince her that she would never have to fight her battles alone again. He was willing and able to devote himself to that particular cause.

"Do you want to tell me about it?" he asked quietly, touching a hand to her hair.

"What?"

She glanced up at him with surprise as well as chagrin.

"Whatever has you frowning so thoughtfully when you should be all smiles," he replied with a half-teasing grin.

Looking away, Kit gave a slight shrug of her shoulders, but she didn't deny the validity of the read he'd taken on her emotions.

"I'm glad the Eastmans are interested in buying the diner. But their time frame is a little tighter than I'd like. I'll have to pack up the apartment, but first I'll have to decide what I want to take with me to Seattle, what I want to sell or give away and what I want to put into storage. Then there's Nathan to consider," she said with a quiver in her voice. "Although he seems to be adjusting to the transition…"

She ducked her head, a catch in he voice, but not before Simon saw the glimmer of tears in her eyes.

"You've had a lot on your plate the past six months, and I know it hasn't been smooth sailing for you, coping on your own. But I hope it's been at least a little easier for you the past couple of weeks—having me here to give you a hand."

Simon kept his tone light, even faintly teasing. He didn't want Kit to feel pressured in any way. Nor did he want to set himself up for too great a fall if she rejected completely the suggestion he was about to make.

"Fishing for a compliment, are you, Simon?" she asked, her own mood brightening perceptively as she responded to him in kind.

"Maybe just a little reassurance that I've been more of a help than a hindrance since I appeared on the scene so unexpectedly," he admitted.

"You've been a lot of help to me, especially since I sprained my ankle. I really appreciate everything you've done for me the past few days."

She tipped her head back and gave him a quick kiss on the chin for emphasis.

"We've worked together pretty well, haven't we?" he continued, his heartbeat accelerating with nervous anticipation.

"Obviously," she murmured with a soft chuckle, feathering tiny kisses along the line his jaw.

"I've been thinking maybe…" He paused, drew a steadying breath, then screwed up his courage and continued in a rush. "Maybe we could continue working together…permanently…if we got married…."

The long, unrelieved silence that followed his proposal spoke unwanted volumes to Simon. So, too, did the way Kit stiffened against him as she turned her face away, making it impossible for him to read her feelings by the expression on her face.

"I don't think we have to do anything that…extreme," she said at last, the flippant tone of her voice totally at odds with her body language. "We'll both be living in Seattle in a few weeks, and we both have Nathan's best interests at heart. We shouldn't have any trouble agreeing on days and times for me to see him."

"Yes, I know, but—" Simon began, then hesitated again.

But what, he wondered. He had offered Kit a proposal of marriage and, bottom line, she had turned him down. Of course, that could have been because he'd made marriage sound more like a solution to a problem than a romantic endeavor.

But if she'd had any interest at all in becoming his wife, wouldn't she have at least given his suggestion some thought instead of dismissing it almost immediately as being *extreme?*

"I know you mean well, Simon," she said, giving him a tender, conciliatory hug. "But we've been thrown together under rather unusual circumstances. Our emotions have been running a lot higher than normal, and a lot of what we've done together has been out of necessity. I care for you, Simon, and I know you care about me, too. But I don't think we have a strong enough foundation on which to build a future."

"I suppose you're right," he agreed, although without any real conviction.

"Trust me, I am."

She hugged him again as she spoke, but still avoided actually looking him in the eye.

They had so much in common, not to mention so much more going for them than many of the couples he knew, Simon thought. But unless, and until, Kit came to that realization, too, she'd continue to reject any arguments he made.

Not that he intended to retreat permanently. He had allowed Lucy to run him off much too easily three years ago, and Kit meant more to him than Lucy ever had. He wasn't about to give up on her—at least not as long as he had even the slightest hope of eventually winning her love and trust.

Right then, right there, just having her curled up in his arms gave him all the incentive he needed to bide his time a while longer.

"Ready to sleep now?" he asked, smoothing a hand down her back to urge her just a little closer.

"I should be. Otherwise, I'll never be able to get up in the morning. But actually…"

She nibbled delicately at his neck, belying, in his mind, at least, the case she'd just made against a lack of foundation. No matter why their paths had crossed again, and no matter how emotional the situation had been, he knew that what they had together was strong and true and very, very real.

Now all he had to do was find a way to make Kit believe it, too.

"Actually?" he prodded, moving his hand from her back to her hip, then to the hot, moist, pulsing place between her thighs.

"Mmm…yes…actually *that*…that's what I really want," she whispered on a sigh.

"And this?" Simon claimed her mouth in a deep, drugging kiss as he teased her with his fingers. "Do you want this, too?"

"Oh, yes, this, too, please…."

"Then you'll have it, Miss Kit, and more…. I promise you…much, much more."

Chapter Fifteen

Kit awoke just after dawn on Saturday morning, a good thirty minutes before the alarm clock on the bedside table was set to go off. Curled close in Simon's protective embrace, she had slept deeply during the night. Her mind as well as her body had been numbed by the grip of sheer exhaustion. But as the faint light of a new day peeked through the lace curtains at the windows, the first thought she had was of Simon's proposal, and her own response to it.

He had stunned her virtually speechless with his suggestion that marriage could be a solution to the problems they faced. In the long, silent moments before she'd formed what she considered a suitable reply, she been tempted—so very, very tempted to agree with him.

But Simon hadn't brought love into the equation. He had been reasonable about the situation and more than practical. But common sense and logic, however admirable, hadn't been enough to sway her. Simon cared for her, of course. She'd acknowledged as much last night. She could also understand how—to his way of thinking, at least—marriage might seem a relatively simple and convenient way to resolve the issue of Nathan's custody.

Had her feelings for Simon been less intense, Kit probably would have agreed with him. But she had fallen in love with him despite all of her increasingly feeble attempts to remain aloof, and she knew that she needed to be loved just as deeply and completely in return. Otherwise Simon's supposedly simple solution—a marriage of convenience—would only bring her heartache in the future.

Kit didn't want to spend her every waking moment fighting what would likely be a losing battle for his attention and affection. Nor did she want to end up in the middle of a nasty divorce when he eventually met someone he *could* love, heart and soul.

Better to maintain her autonomy, she had concluded. Even the voracity of their lovemaking before they'd finally slept hadn't changed her mind. She still believed they would both be happier in the long run on their own instead of tied to each other only because of Nathan.

As she had told Simon, there were other ways to share custody of his son, especially since they'd be living in the same city. She also trusted that he would never cut her out completely even though he would probably have the legal right to do so. She would rather start as she would likely end up going eventually anyway—on the sidelines of Simon Gilmore's life, not center stage.

Being careful not to disturb him since he was still sleeping soundly, Kit slipped out of bed; gathered fresh underwear, jeans and a T-shirt; and hobbled to the bathroom to take a shower. Then, to return the favor Simon had done for her earlier in the week, she headed for the kitchen, started a pot of coffee brewing and put together the ingredients for a batch of pancakes. She might not be much of a cook overall, but years of watching her mother in action had taught her a few basic tricks.

Simon was awake but still in bed when she joined him in the bedroom again. Catching a glimpse of his face a few moments before he heard her approach, Kit noted his troubled expression. The lines furrowing his forehead smoothed quickly, however, as he turned his head on the pillow and looked at her.

"You're up early," he commented with a welcoming smile as he pushed up against the bed pillows piled behind his head. "Mmm…and you've made coffee, too."

Kit offered him one of the white china mugs she held, then sat down on the edge of the mattress.

"Good thing I'm up because you've been a real sleepy-head."

She smiled, too, then took a tentative sip of her coffee.

"I can't imagine why."

Simon's smile turned sexy and his eyes glinted with mischief. He could be so charming with so little effort, making it all but impossible for her to keep from falling under his spell. Luckily for her, knowing what he was all about was half the battle.

"I'm sure you'll come up with a good reason once you give it a little thought," she said with wry good humor.

"Oh, I've been giving *it* quite a bit of thought. Unfortunately, I have a feeling that's all I'm going to be able to give *it* this morning since you're already dressed. Unless there's a chance that I can somehow entice you into getting naked with me again," he teased.

"No chance at all," she advised him primly, standing again, out of his reach, just to be on the safe side.

Giving in to Simon would have been all too easy. The pleasure of his passionate lovemaking could very well become addictive. But having sex with him while she was still trying to shore up her emotional defenses would only cause her more confusion.

Kit wasn't about to avoid completely the joy of being physically intimate with him. She didn't have that much willpower yet. Weaning herself away from him gradually, starting immediately, seemed like a good idea, though. She had to prepare for the day when she would no longer be a part of Simon's, and Nathan's, everyday life. Otherwise, the pain of losing them would be more than she'd be able to bear.

"I meant to tell you yesterday that my parents want us to come out to the ranch tomorrow," Simon said, obviously taking her cue and easily switching gears. "I told them I'd have to check with you first to make sure you didn't have other plans."

"None at all," Kit assured him, then glanced at the clock. "I'd better get back to the kitchen. I have pancake batter ready to ladle onto the griddle."

"I'm going to take a quick shower. Then I'll get Nathan up, okay?"

"Okay."

Kit allowed her gaze to linger on Simon a moment longer, locking into her memory the sight of his bare, muscular chest; his dark, sleep-tousled, curly hair; and his bright, gentle, smiling blue eyes. Then she turned to head back to the kitchen, a plan taking shape in her mind.

She could torment herself with flights of fancy and impossible dreams a while longer, or she could face reality and take action accordingly. Simon's bond with Nathan was now a solid one. All she really needed to do now was let him take over as primary caregiver, 24/7.

Kit had long since decided not to fight Simon for legal custody of Nathan. Seeing him with his son, she truly believed that he and Nathan belonged together. She also now believed that the time had finally come for her presence in the little boy's life to gradually diminish. That process could begin any time now, even as early as tomorrow—as long as her courage didn't fail her.

Hearing the shower go on in the bathroom, Kit thought of Simon standing naked under the spray of steamy water. With a pang of longing so intense her breath caught in her throat and her eyes welled with tears, she also thought of how much she loved him and how much she wanted him and his son in her life forever. Then she set the griddle on the stove, lit the burner underneath it and reminded herself, sadly, that wanting something didn't always mean you'd actually get it.

Had Kit needed any additional spur to follow through with her plan, she got it in spades Saturday afternoon. Just after the busy lunch hour rush, as she, Bonnie and Sara cleared tables and loaded the diner's dishwasher, Cassie Holden of Mountain View Realtors stopped by with a buyer's contract for the Dinner Belle property.

Kit had been expecting the Eastmans to make an offer, but not quite so soon. She also hadn't thought that their initial offer would be so close to her asking price that quibbling would be foolish. They were prepared to pay in cash, as well, thus eliminating the wait to have a mortgage approved. They required only one agreement on her part to seal the deal. They insisted on taking possession of the diner and the upstairs apartment in no more than four weeks' time.

Sitting across the table from Cassie, Kit read through the simple contract with a surprising sense of sadness. She was about to sell the only home she'd ever had—a place that held for her mostly happy memories. She would also be cutting her strongest tie to the small town of Belle— the place where she'd grown from young girl to independent woman.

But she had decided years ago that she wanted more out of life than the Dinner Belle Diner could offer her, and Seattle wasn't that far away, after all. She could return to Belle occasionally any time she wanted to.

"You don't have to sign the contract today," Cassie advised, obviously sensing her momentary hesitation. "I told the Eastmans you might want to think about it over the weekend, and they didn't have any problem with that. They understand that this is a really big decision for you to have to make. They want you to be sure about it before you agree to sell them the diner."

Kit had been sure about selling the Dinner Belle from the day she'd contacted Cassie about listing the property. Despite the lingering ache in her heart for times past, she was still sure about it now.

"I *have* thought about it—a lot. Their offer seems more than fair to me and I don't foresee having any problem turning the place over to them on July 15 as they've asked."

Kit took her pen from the pocket of her apron, and refusing to allow herself any second thoughts, she signed her name with a quick flourish on the line provided.

"I wish I could deal with all my clients so easily," Cassie said as Kit slid the contract across the table to her.

"I was ready to sell and the Eastmans were ready to buy, and you've been an excellent facilitator."

Amazingly enough, she felt relieved to have the deal done.

"I appreciate the compliment."

"Do you know if the Eastmans have any experience running a diner?" Kit asked as Cassie folded the contract and tucked it into her tote.

"I'm thinking probably not," Cassie replied, shooting Kit a wry smile.

"I'd be more than happy to give them some pointers over the next few weeks."

"I have a feeling they'd really appreciate that."

"Tell them to come in on Monday morning. The sooner we get started, the better they'll get to know George and Bonnie and Sara, and the more confident they'll feel taking over on their own in July."

"I'll do that," Cassie replied. Standing along with Kit, the real-estate agent picked up her tote and slung the straps over her shoulder. "I'll also see that you get a copy of the contract Monday morning, as well."

"Thanks a lot, Cassie."

"Thank *you,* Kit."

Watching the agent walk to the diner's front door, Kit drew a deep, steadying breath. She was certain that she'd made the right decision, and with her signature on the buyer's contract, it was a good thing.

Kit was about to return to the kitchen when Isaac Woodrow strode purposefully into the diner, pausing only long enough to hold the door open for Cassie. Kit hadn't seen or spoken to her attorney since the day she'd met with him,

Simon and John Mahoney at his office almost two weeks ago. But then, there had been no real need to get in touch with him.

"Isaac, it's nice to see you," she said by way of greeting. "Have you come for a late lunch?"

"It's nice to see you, too, Kit. I take it all has been going well for you. No problems with Mr. Gilmore?" he asked, his tone as probing as the look in his eyes as he met her gaze.

"No problems at all."

"That's good to hear. *Very* good."

Kit gestured to an empty table and asked again, "Would you like to have some lunch or not?"

"Not," he said with noticeable regret, though he did take a seat at the table. "My wife has me on a diet. She fed me salad for lunch. *Salad…*" He shook his head in disgust, then nodded to an empty chair. "Can we talk for a few minutes?"

"Of course," she agreed, her heart rate accelerating as a jittery sensation roiled through her stomach. "Is something wrong, Isaac?"

"Not necessarily." He took an envelope from the pocket of his faded denim shirt. "Especially if you and Mr. Gilmore have gotten to be on good terms where Nathan's concerned. I've assumed that was the case since I haven't heard from you or his attorney since our meeting, and since I've also seen you together on several occasions."

"Yes, Simon and I have been on good terms lately," Kit acknowledged, mentally cursing the blush that heated her cheeks.

In a small town like Belle, it was no surprise that her relationship with Simon had been noted by her attorney, not to mention by anyone else with two good eyes to see. She had no reason to be embarrassed, either. They were both consenting adults and they had always behaved appropriately in public.

But Kit had never liked having the feeling that her life was an open book easily read by everyone in town.

"Well, then, that should make the test results from the lab in Missoula good news to you." Isaac unfolded the letter he'd received and handed it to her as he added, "Simon Gilmore is definitely Nathan Kane's father. Not that I imagine you've had any doubts about it."

"Actually, no doubts at all," Kit admitted, glancing at the letter, then setting it aside.

"You do understand and accept that as Nathan's father, Mr. Gilmore will likely be given full custody of his son. We can challenge him in court, of course, but I'd be remiss not to warn you that the most you could hope for is a visitation order. I'm thinking that under the circumstances, you and Mr. Gilmore ought to be able to work something out on your own, though."

"Yes, I'm sure we can."

Offering the attorney a reassuring smile, Kit refolded the letter and handed it back to him.

She had expected all along that the DNA test results would prove without a doubt Simon's paternity. But she hadn't anticipated feeling such a strange sense of loss upon actually hearing the news.

Her place in Nathan's life had shifted irreversibly. Starting very soon now, her access to the little boy she loved as her own would be dependent on her ability to stay in Simon's good graces. Married to him or not, she'd have no real guarantee that he would always feel fondly toward her—especially if he met a woman he could love as much as he'd once loved Lucy.

"I'll go ahead and prepare the necessary documents to nonsuit your petition for adoption, then," Isaac advised, standing as he tucked the letter into his pocket again. "I'll also have Margie send you a check refunding the balance in your trust account."

"Thanks, Isaac, for all your help." Kit stood, too, and offered her hand in farewell.

"My pleasure, Kit." He shook her hand, than gave her a courtly bow. "Good luck to you." He hesitated for a long moment, then added, "Any truth to the rumor you've found a buyer for the Dinner Belle?"

"News sure does travel fast around this town," Kit mused with a wry smile. "And yes, it's true. The new owners will be taking over in mid-July."

"What will you do then?"

"Go back to Seattle, finish graduate school and hopefully get a job."

She smiled brightly as she attempted to make her future sound like an adventure waiting to happen.

"Ah, the joys of youth." Isaac smiled, too, a wistful look in his eyes, but only for an instant. "You have a good life ahead of you, Kit Davenport. Just don't be a stranger around here, okay?"

"Okay, Isaac. You take care."

"You, too, Kit."

Once again Kit started back to the kitchen, stopping to clear a table of plates, glass and silverware along the way. Only a few customers remained in the diner, but they would be gone soon. Then she'd have to tell Bonnie, Sara and George that she'd sold the diner.

She would have to tell Simon, too—not only about selling the diner, but also about Isaac's visit. Not a difficult task since both bits of news were good. She'd have the money she needed to continue her education as she'd hoped, and he would have his son, free and clear.

There was no reason to get all teary-eyed. Everything was working out for the best for everyone involved. Nothing stayed the same forever. Change was good. One door closed, and another opened.

Yeah, right, pile on the platitudes, Kit told herself, rubbing her eyes with her free hand. That will help a lot.

"Hey, Kit, are you okay?" Bonnie asked, catching sight of her as she walked into the kitchen.

"Got something in my eye," she lied. "Otherwise, I'm just fine. I also have news—good news for all of us. I've sold the Dinner Belle Diner…."

Chapter Sixteen

In the time that passed from early Saturday morning until nearly noon on Sunday, Kit seemed to Simon more and more like a woman on a mission. Not a bad thing in and of itself, he acknowledged. But he didn't have the first clue about what was driving her. Nor did he have any idea of what her ultimate purpose might be.

Saturday afternoon Kit had told him about the contract she'd signed, effectively setting in motion the sale of the Dinner Belle Diner to Earl and Sylvie Eastman. She had also told him about the visit she'd had from Isaac Woodrow and his news about the DNA test results, unaware that John Mahoney had given him the same information via a telephone call.

Her manner toward him had been brisker and more businesslike than it had been for the past few days. Such behavior had always been a part of her nature, especially when she had quandaries to address. She had a lot to do in order to be ready to turn over the diner to the Eastman couple in mid-July. She also had decisions to make regarding her relationship with him, as well as Nathan.

At least her passion for him hadn't cooled in any noticeable way. In bed with him last night, Kit had been just as greedy as he—perhaps even more so—for the lovemaking they'd shared in the deep night darkness.

Her physical response to him had given Simon a small measure of hope that she might reconsider his marriage proposal. But he had also begun to feel as if they were no longer on the same page, emotionally—if they ever really had been initially. The distance she seemed determined to put between them had him fighting uncertainty on the one hand and frustration on the other as the time when they'd planned to leave for the ranch approached.

Since Friday night Simon had told himself that by continuing to treat Kit with attentive care he would eventually win her trust in his love. But suddenly there seemed to be an invisible wall around her, deflecting his every attempt to intensify the bond he'd thought they already shared. Though she wasn't totally unreceptive to him, causing him to question his perceptions, the gradually increasing chill in her overall demeanor baffled him completely.

Stacking the dishwasher with the dishes from the early lunch they'd shared, as Nathan played happily enough in his high chair with a set of measuring cups and spoons, Simon tried to decide what to do next. He could have come right out and confronted Kit any of the half-dozen times that her behavior had seemed to him just a little off-kilter.

But the attempt he'd made to talk to her openly and honestly about marriage Friday night hadn't worked in his favor at all. In fact, he had begun to believe that if only he had kept his mouth shut and waited a while longer, instead, to propose to her, he would have been much better off by far.

The thump of yet another drawer closing in Nathan's bedroom caught Simon's attention. He closed the door of the dishwasher and turned the dial to start it running. Then he released Nathan from his high chair, and holding him by the hand, went to find out what Kit was up to.

She had said something about getting a few things together to take with them to the ranch when she'd left him to tidy up the kitchen. By the sounds he'd heard, however, it seemed to him like she was packing up a lot more than his son's diaper bag.

"Hey, Kit…what are you doing in here?" Simon asked.

As he paused in the bedroom doorway, his gaze landed with gut-twisting accuracy on the open suitcase, almost full of Nathan's clothes, Kit had set on the changing table.

"Kit? What doing, Kit? What doing?" Nathan demanded, as well.

Running over to her, the little boy tugged on the leg of her jeans to get her attention.

"Hey, guys," she said.

She flashed them a bright smile that didn't quite make it to her pale eyes. Studiously avoiding Simon's gaze altogether, she stooped to gather Nathan into her arms, then nuzzled him on the neck.

"Ready to go to your grandma's house?"

"Go Gahma's house?" he repeated, rocking excitedly in her arms. "Go Gahma's house *now*, Kit?"

"In just a few minutes." She set him down again with obvious reluctance, then instructed, "Go get your teddy bear, okay, little buddy?"

"'Kay, Kit."

He toddled across the bedroom to his bed, then got down on all fours and crawled under to retrieve his favorite stuffed animal from where it had fallen earlier.

Eyeing Kit steadily as she turned away to close the suitcase, Simon moved to stand beside her. With a growing sense of trepidation, he gently touched her arm, then gave it a tug, determined to get her attention as he repeated his question.

"What are you doing, Kit?"

"I'm getting Nathan's clothes together so you'll have them out at the ranch." Still she refused to look directly at him. Instead she tipped her head to a cardboard box on the floor that he hadn't noticed yet. "I've packed up most of his toys, too. You can take them with you today, as well."

"Why would I want to do that?"

Growing more confused and frustrated by the minute, Simon took his hand from Kit's arm, but only so that he could grasp her by the shoulders and turn her so that she had no choice but to face him squarely. She wouldn't look him in the eye, though—not until he tucked a finger under her chin and tipped her face up.

The anguish he saw in her lovely eyes, edged as it was with defiance, not only caught him by surprise, but also filled him with instant, and unaccountable, dread.

"You're more than ready to take over Nathan's care on your own, full-time now, Simon, and today seems like as good a day as any for you to get started. It's also time that I began playing a more secondary role in his life. We've gotten the DNA test results, and you're undoubtedly his father. Since I've asked Isaac to withdraw my petition for adoption, you shouldn't have any problems at all gaining legal custody of him. In fact, I doubt it will entail more than our signatures on some court documents."

The blithe tone Kit used belied so completely the look Simon saw in her eyes that it gave him pause.

Was this moment as painful for her as he wanted to believe it was? Or had he totally misjudged her feelings over the past two weeks, not only for Nathan, but also for him? Was it really possible that she could let both of them go so easily?

He didn't want to think so, but she wasn't giving him much of a choice. Remembering the way they'd made love Saturday night didn't even offer him any reassurance. Yes, passion had run high between them, yet he had sensed a certain reserve about her that he hadn't noticed previously.

Kit had seemed to enjoy the physical pleasure, but she had also seemed to keep her emotions in check, refusing to engage with him on a deeper, more meaningful level. He had tried to ignore the hurt he'd felt then, but that was impossible to do now.

"So you're ready to let me take custody of Nathan, just like that?" Simon demanded with a snap of his fingers for emphasis.

His voice sounded much harsher than he'd intended, but at least he'd managed to maintain some control over his roiling emotions. More than anything, he wanted to grab her by the shoulders again and give her a good shake in a last-ditch effort to make her see sense.

But such an act would be rooted as much in anger as in pain. Likely it would only cause her to feel even more mistrustful toward him than she already seemed to be.

"That's been the goal all along, hasn't it?" she asked, her confusion seeming feigned to him. "You hired an expensive attorney to plead your case to the court. You agreed to paternity tests. You've spent the past couple of weeks learning to care for Nathan. You made it known that you intend to be the one to raise him. That's exactly what you're going to be able to do now, without any more muss or fuss from me."

The smile Kit offered him was so bright, so cheerful and so damned guileless that for a long moment Simon was totally at a loss for words. She had ceded the battle while at the same time she'd clearly and concisely pointed out how pleased he should be because he'd gotten exactly what he'd wanted.

Only he hadn't—at least to his way of thinking.

"What about you?" he asked at last. "Or more precisely, what about you and me?"

"Oh, hey, you don't have to worry about me," she said, turning away to snap the clasps on the suitcase. "I'm okay with the situation—really okay. I know how much you love Nathan, and seeing you with him, I know you're going to be a wonderful father. As for you and me, I'm sure we'll be able to work out a visitation schedule once we're back in Seattle. By then I'm sure Nathan will be able to think of me as just another friend come to visit you."

"So this is it, Kit?" He gazed at her with disbelief as he tried to understand what she'd said to him. "You don't want to see either one of us again here in Belle?"

"I know you have to get back to work at the paper within the next couple of weeks. Before you can do that you're going to have to get Nathan settled in his new home and arrange for childcare," she calmly pointed out. "I have less than four weeks to give Earl and Sylvie Eastman a short course in diner operation, plus pack up and move out of here myself. It's also probably a good idea for me to stay out of the way for a few weeks so you and Nathan can establish routines of your own without having me in the picture at all."

"Obviously you've given a lot of thought to this whole…transition. The only thing you haven't done is ask *me* how I feel about *your* plans. You know, Kit Davenport, you're a hell of a lot more like Lucy Kane than I imagined, and I don't mean that as a compliment."

"I'm sorry you feel that way, Simon," she replied, though she sounded more defensive than contrite. "I guess I just assumed you were thinking along the same lines."

"Well, I wasn't, but I certainly am now. I can't see any sense in forcing you to put up with any more muss or fuss from *me* or my son," he shot back with a sudden, final flare of anger that faded almost immediately into regret and remorse.

"It's best this way, Simon," Kit said, her voice now sounding strained.

"Yeah, well, I guess I'll have to take your word for it, won't I?"

Unable to argue with her any further, Simon reached around her, grabbed the handle of the suitcase and lifted it off the changing table. Then he said to Nathan, "Ready to go, little buddy?"

"Ready go, Dahee. Go Gahma's now?"

"Yes, son, we're going to Grandma's house now."

"Kit go Gahma's, too, Dahee? Kit go?"

Clutching his teddy bear, Nathan ran to Kit and held up his arms to her in invitation.

She lifted him into her arms and hugged him close, the renewed look of anguish in her eyes almost undoing

Simon's steely resolve. Maybe she wasn't as sure of the choices she'd made as she'd tried to make him believe. But maybe he'd only be setting himself up for more rejection if he challenged her again now. Maybe if he let her live with her decision for a while, she'd realize what a mistake she was making by shutting him out of her life. Maybe then she'd be willing to give him another chance to prove how much he loved her.

"No, I'm not going with you today, big boy. Just you and your daddy are going to Grandma's house. I have to work," Kit said.

That Nathan understood.

"Bye, bye, Kit...bye, bye...?"

"Yes, sweetie...bye, bye."

Simon easily hefted the cardboard box of toys under his arm. Carrying Nathan, Kit followed after him as he made his way down the staircase and out the side door of the diner.

He didn't dare look at her as he loaded the suitcase and the box into the back of the SUV and she secured Nathan into his car seat. He wanted to be angry with her for behaving in such a cavalier manner. But all he could feel just then was very, very sad.

Despite all that they had shared over the past two weeks, she still seemed determined to send him away, and he wasn't about to beg her to let him stay. He'd much rather give her a chance to think about what she'd done. There was some sorting out he needed to do, as well. Perhaps after a time out, she might be ready to reconsider his proposal if, in fact, he wanted to offer it again.

Maybe her take on the situation was more accurate than his was. Then again, he temporized, noting the way her shoulders slumped, as she stood with him beside the SUV in the brilliant afternoon sunlight, maybe not.

"Take care of yourself, Simon, and Nathan, too," she said, extending her hand to him in polite farewell. "I'll be in touch as soon as I'm settled again in Seattle."

Instead of merely shaking her hand as she seemed to expect him to do, Simon grasped it firmly, then pulled her into his arms. Giving her no opportunity to voice any protest, he kissed her almost roughly, not to mention nearly breathless, smack on the mouth.

"You take good care, too, Kit," he growled in her ear.

She trembled despite the warmth of the air and leaned against him with seeming weakness for a long moment. Tightening his hold on her just a little, Simon allowed himself a small, secret smile.

Oh, yes, she would be doing some thinking in the days ahead, he acknowledged, allowing himself only a glimpse of her startled expression before he climbed into the SUV, shut the door on her and started the engine. Now all he had to do was hope that her thoughts about their having a future together would finally, and firmly, mesh with his.

Kit stood on the sidewalk outside the Dinner Belle, arms crossed over her chest, watching sadly as Simon drove away. Somewhere in the back of her mind she hadn't really believed she'd be able to run him off so easily. She hadn't factored in the possibility that she would be capable of playing her self-assigned part so well.

Not that getting Simon to go along with the decisions she'd made for the two of them had been a snap, because it hadn't been. But secretly she had hoped that he would refuse to do her bidding altogether. After all, Friday night he *had* talked about marrying her.

Perverse as she knew it was under the circumstances that *she* had created, Kit felt as if he'd abandoned her, just as she'd thought for so long that he'd once abandoned Lucy. In fact, she had only gotten what she'd said that she wanted.

She could finally understand the bitter tears Lucy had shed after he'd left her three years ago. As Simon had accused her so angrily only a few minutes ago, *she* had treated him just as Lucy had done. She had made choices that involved both of them, and though he wouldn't know it, she had lied to him, as well, by pretending that she didn't want to have a permanent, committed relationship with him.

Now bitter tears welled in *her* eyes as she turned to go back inside the diner. Remorseful as Lucy had temporarily been about sending Simon away, she at least had had the comfort of knowing that he loved her. Kit knew only that she had derailed his simple solution to a custody issue that had never really existed—a solution she was sure he'd come up with merely out of a sense of obligation to her for all she'd done to keep his son safe.

Better to cut the cord all at once on her own, though, than to live with the fear of having it cut for her when Simon fell in love with someone else, Kit told herself for the umpteenth time as she closed the apartment door. Unfortunately, the emptiness of the space she'd so recently and so happily shared with Simon and his son weighed on her much too heavily for her to really believe her own caution.

Maybe she should have accepted the affection Simon

had to offer her and been grateful. Maybe she should have been glad that he'd been willing to give her the chance to help him raise his son. Maybe her love for him would have been enough to make a marriage between them work. Maybe even, eventually, he would have grown to love her, too. Then again, maybe not, but one way or another, she had lost the opportunity to know for sure.

Unless, of course, that last kiss he'd given her hadn't merely been his way of saying goodbye....

Pressing her fingertips to her lips, still slightly swollen from the intensity of that very kiss, Kit wanted to believe that he'd only intended to add a bit of drama to their farewell. His kiss hello the first day he'd walked into the diner had been equally startling and almost as brusque. How better to end what he'd started than in a similar manner?

Only, the first time Simon had kissed her he hadn't used his teeth or his tongue to make her go weak in the knees—

"Enough," she ordered, her voice echoing harshly in the silence surrounding her.

She could moon about Simon Gilmore or she could brace up and busy herself with something constructive, such as all the packing she had to do. Brushing away the tears that had trickled down her cheeks despite her best effort to keep them in check, Kit looked around the living room, trying to decide where to begin the monumental task she had ahead of her. She had not only her own belongings to sort out, but also things of her mother's as well as things of Lucy's she hadn't yet had the heart to give away.

Of course, her gaze *would* fall first on the only two items in the room that weren't a part of her property, or her mother's, or Lucy's, or even Nathan's, but rather Simon's. On the table beside the sofa, obviously forgotten by him in his haste to leave—or more honestly, the haste she had imposed on him to leave—sat his laptop computer and 35 mm camera.

Immediately she thought of all the other things he'd likely left behind, drawn as if by a magnet to her bedroom. There she found some of his clothing folded neatly in his open overnight bag. A half-empty box of condoms remained on the nightstand beside the unmade bed, a mess of twisted sheets and tumbled pillows.

The ache in Kit's heart swelled to an almost unbearable level as she turned and fled down the hallway, but she couldn't escape his presence altogether. In the bathroom, she saw his toothbrush hanging in the holder beside hers, and his razor, can of shaving cream and bottle of spicy aftershave sat side by side on the countertop.

She hurried into Nathan's room. No sign of Simon there, but her anguish shifted and then blossomed in a new and equally devastating direction. Simon wasn't the only one she had sent away, perhaps forever. Nathan wouldn't be coming home to her here again, either. But the bed he'd slept in so many nights still awaited him, as did the rocking chair where she'd sat with him, looking at picture books. And the dresser that had once held his clothes, and the toy box, were empty now, too—as empty as her heart.

Slowly Kit walked back to her bedroom, tears blurring her eyes all over again. She sat on the edge of the bed, too bereft to do anything but clutch a pillow still scented with the spicy tang of Simon's aftershave and weep.

She had been certain that sending him away with Nathan had been the right thing to do for all of them. A marriage without mutual love would eventually be no marriage at all. She'd meant only to save them both from future animosity.

Surely a choice made only to help shouldn't hurt so much. But it did, she thought as she curled up on the bed, her sobbing unabated—it hurt almost more than she could bear.

Chapter Seventeen

"What can I get for you today, Mrs. Averill?" Kit asked, pausing beside the elderly woman's table on Wednesday morning.

Business had been brisk since she'd opened the Dinner Belle as usual at seven o'clock. But there was a bit of a lull now as there normally was between the last of the breakfast crowd finishing up and the first folks coming in ready for lunch.

"Two eggs over easy, hash-brown potatoes, bacon and a couple of biscuits, same as always," Winifred replied.

"We have huckleberry pancakes on special today, made with the first fresh berries of the season," Kit advised her, aware that Mrs. Averill never bothered to look at the menu.

"Well, then, give me a short stack of pancakes instead of the biscuits. I do so love fresh huckleberries."

"That's what I thought," Kit said. "Let me give George your order, then I'll be right back with your coffee."

Mrs. Averill caught her by the arm as she was about to turn away, halting her in midstride.

"I heard you sold the Dinner Belle to people from Texas," Winifred said with the barest hint of displeasure.

"Yes, I did. The new owners are Earl and Sylvie Eastman. They *are* from Texas, but they've spent a lot of time in Montana the past ten years or so. They'll be moving into the upstairs apartment and taking over the diner in three weeks. They're very nice people, Mrs. Averill, and they're very excited about running the Dinner Belle. They're going to let George, Bonnie and Sara stay on, too, so no one will be jobless—except me, of course." Kit smiled so that Mrs. Averill would know that was all right with her, then added politely, "They're in the kitchen right now getting some pointers from George. Would you like to meet them?"

"Maybe another time." Winifred still held on to Kit's arm, refusing to let her go just yet. "Tell me, what are you planning to do once the Texans take over around here?"

"What I've planned to do all along—go back to Seattle, finish my graduate work, then get a job with social services," she explained.

Though she schooled herself to be patient with the elderly woman, she was suddenly eager to get away from her and her all-too-probing, not to mention all-too-knowing, gaze.

"I didn't see young Simon Gilmore's fancy black SUV parked out front when I came in earlier. I was hoping he'd be waiting tables again today. He looked darn cute in that frilly white apron Bonnie Lennox conned him into wearing when he was helping out here last week after you sprained your ankle," Winifred chortled.

"He's out at the Double Bar S with Nathan. He wanted to spend a few days with his parents before he heads back to Seattle with his son," Kit explained, amazed at how off-hand her voice sounded.

Talking about Simon and Nathan hurt just about as much as thinking about them, and that was all she'd done since Sunday afternoon. She had wondered if they were missing her the same way she was missing them. Evidently not, she'd sadly concluded, since Simon hadn't called her once in almost three days, not even to make arrangements to pick up the personal belongings he'd left at the apartment.

"Then you'll all be going back there together?"

"Well, no, not together."

"Rumor had it you two were something of an item only a few days ago," Winifred said, eyeing her pointedly.

"Rumors aren't always based on fact," Kit pointed out, trying, unsuccessfully, to ease her arm from Mrs. Averill's grasp.

She did not want to discuss her relationship with Simon, past, present or future. Especially since they had no relationship at present, and likely wouldn't have one worth mentioning in the future.

"He was staying with you in the apartment upstairs, helping you out with the boy, as well as the diner, while you were laid up with a bum ankle, wasn't he?"

"Well, yes, he was, but I don't really think that's enough to make us an item," Kit insisted.

"It is by my reckoning. The man put on an apron and waited tables for you, Miss Kit. Not many men I know of would have done that for a woman unless she meant something special to him. Most men tend to show how much they care about you by how they act, instead. The way he was acting the past couple of weeks, Simon Gilmore sure seemed to me to be a man in love. But it sounds to me like maybe you ran him off," Mrs. Averill pointed out none too gently.

"I didn't run him off," Kit shot back defensively, though she knew, in fact, that she had.

But she'd been having a hard time rationalizing her behavior to herself the past few days. Trying to explain her reasoning to Winifred Averill would be well nigh impossible. Nor would it do her the least bit of good. The woman had already pointed out she'd made a big mistake, and Kit had to agree with her there.

"I can't think of any other reason why he would take that little boy of his back to Seattle and leave you here alone. He doesn't seem to me to be the kind who'd just up and go unless he felt he had no other choice."

"Maybe I'm the one who had no other choice," Kit said in a strained voice. "Maybe I needed more than I thought he could give me."

"Because he didn't snow you with a lot of pretty words?" Mrs. Averill prodded. "Men can't always say how they feel, but they sure as hell know how to show it."

As Simon had shown *her* so many times over the past two weeks, Kit thought with dismay. Unfortunately, she'd been so defensive toward him that she hadn't realized it until now. Although he'd never *said* that he loved her, the tender care with which he'd treated her had spoken volumes she'd been too foolish to acknowledge.

She must have looked as stricken as she felt as she met Winifred Averill's unwavering gaze. The elderly woman gave her arm a reassuring squeeze before she finally let her go.

"We have to make decisions every day of our lives,"

Winifred said kindly. "Sometimes we make the right one up front, and sometimes we don't. We usually know when we've made a mistake, and if we're lucky we'll get the chance to decide again, and maybe get it right the second time around. Seems to me, Miss Kit, you might want to consider your options and decide what to do next." With a nod of satisfaction, she sat back in her chair and made a shooing motion with her hand. "Now run along and put in my breakfast order while old George still has some of his huckleberry pancake batter ready to slap on the griddle."

"Yes, ma'am, I'll put your order in right now," Kit said, glad to finally be released from the elderly woman's well-meaning company.

"Don't forget to bring me some coffee, too. Giving advice has left me just a little bit parched."

"No, ma'am, I won't."

Kit spent the rest of the day thinking about what Winifred Averill had said to her. In fact, she was so distracted that she got orders confused, dropped silverware on the floor and knocked over a fresh pitcher of iced tea, spilling it on the counter.

She earned a lot of teasing from Bonnie and Sara, though they were gentler with her than they could have been. They, too, were aware of Simon's departure over the weekend. And while they hadn't pressed her for details, they had to have noticed her less-than-cheerful demeanor the past couple of days.

Kit did muster enough good humor to explain to Earl and Sylvie that she'd been demonstrating how *not* to serve customers efficiently and they, in turn, seemed to appreciate her attempt at levity. She didn't mind making the effort. They were such nice people. Still, by the time the

Dinner Belle closed for the day, she was very glad to be alone at last.

Upstairs in the apartment, however, Kit paced from room to room to room, unable to relax. She hadn't been sleeping very well at all, as evidenced by the dark shadows under her eyes. But she was too restless to take a nap.

She could have packed a few boxes—she'd hardly made a dent in all that she needed to do before mid-July. But her thoughts were as scattered as they had been down in the diner, making it almost impossible for her to focus on even the most undemanding task.

She considered walking down to the park as she had done the past two afternoons on the off chance that Simon would be there with Nathan. But she knew he didn't have to make a trip to town to entertain his son out-of-doors. She had seen the sturdy wooden jungle gym, complete with slide, swings and a small fort, that his parents had erected, turning the lawn into a perfect play area for the little boy.

She could call Simon, of course, and remind him of the clothes, laptop computer and camera he'd left at her apartment. Kit had been sure that he would have missed his belongings by now, especially his computer and expensive camera. But that didn't seem to be the case.

Was he so busy that he couldn't make time to see her even for the few minutes it would take him to stop by for his stuff? More importantly, didn't he and Nathan miss her even a little bit? Was it possible that they'd forgotten all about her in so short a time?

Kit had been fully prepared for a desperate telephone call from Simon on Sunday night—a call to tell her that Nathan was so distraught at being separated from her that he wouldn't settle down to sleep. But the call hadn't come, and she'd realized, eventually, that the little boy had gotten used to staying with different people in his young life.

Nathan had also formed an almost instant bond of love and trust with Simon. As long as the little boy had his daddy close by, Kit knew that he would be content. With doting grandparents also added to the mix, he was probably as happy as he could be.

Eyeing Simon's overnight bag, now packed with his clothes and other personal items, his laptop computer and camera stacked in a corner of the living room, Kit admitted that the time had come for her do something, anything, to end the stalemate between them. Pacing and fretting and pacing some more benefited her not at all.

She had to do what Winifred Averill had advised that morning. She had to make another decision, one that just might counteract the awful choice she'd made on Sunday afternoon. She could call Simon and ask him to come get his belongings, but that would make her a supplicant of sorts.

She needed to take action in a different, more empowering way. She had to gather her courage, drive out to the ranch and confront him from a position of strength, ready, as she was, to put her heart on the line. Nothing less would do after the way she'd rejected him.

And if he really wasn't interested in her, if he didn't love her as she hoped? Then she would return to town, head held high, knowing that she had done what she could, and prepare herself to make yet another, perhaps more rewarding decision.

Her mind made up, Kit slung her purse strap over her shoulder, grabbed her car keys, then managed somehow to roll Simon's overnight bag down the staircase while juggling the lightweight computer and bulky camera in her arms. She couldn't open the side door of the diner with her hands full, however. Deciding that she'd better stow the overnight bag in her car, then come back for the computer and camera, she set them on one of the steps.

Turning to the door again, Kit unlocked it, swung it open and gasped with surprise. Simon stood on the threshold, key in hand, holding Nathan in his arms, an equally startled look on his face. She stared at him wordlessly, un-. comprehending at first. Then Nathan shrieked excitedly, breaking the spell that had held her still.

"Kit…Kit…Dahee see Kit? Miss you, Kit…Nafan miss you berry much."

The little boy held out his arms to her. She let go of the overnight bag's handle and took him from Simon, hugging him close, tears filling her eyes and spilling unhindered onto her cheeks.

"Oh, baby…sweet baby boy, I've missed you, too," she sobbed, nuzzling his soft, dark curls.

"Dahee, Kit cwying," Nathan said as he reached up and patted her gently on the face.

"I know, son."

"Don't cwy, Kit," Nathan begged, a quiver in his voice.

"I'm sorry, sweetie, but I can't seem to stop. Just give me another minute, okay?"

"'Kay…"

She took a deep breath, trying to steady herself. Then she felt the touch of Simon's hand on her hair. Meeting his searching gaze, she willed herself to rein in her runaway emotions, but still her tears continued to flow.

Simon stood by helplessly, unsure what to say or do. He had been shocked by how sad and utterly exhausted Kit looked when she opened the door to him so unexpectedly. He had meant to let himself into the diner, then call up to her so as not to give her a scare. But he'd caught her as she was about to leave, uncannily timing his arrival with her own departure.

He knew he should have called first, but he hadn't wanted to give her a chance to put him off. Although that seemed unlikely now, the way she was holding on to Nathan and sobbing almost uncontrollably.

"Hey, are you all right?" he asked after another moment's hesitation, speaking to her in a gentle tone.

"No, but give me a few minutes, and I will be." Looking away, she dug a tissue from the pocket of her jeans and made a futile stab at wiping away the tears still spilling from her eyes. "It's just that I've missed you so much, you and Nathan, and seeing you here…these are happy tears. Believe me, they really are."

"Would it help if I told you that we've missed you, too? Because we have…quite a lot, in fact," Simon admitted.

"Well, you couldn't prove it by me. You've stayed away three whole days," Kit said.

She stared at him accusingly, then hiccuped, giggled for a moment and started to cry all over again.

"Kit, Kit, Kit," he chided her softly, putting an arm around her shoulders and drawing her close to his side, Nathan and all. "What am I going to do with you?"

"I don't know, Simon," she replied, leaning her head against his chest. "I'm such a mess."

Simon hadn't wanted to distance himself from Kit so completely the past few days, but he'd forced himself to do it. He had been determined to stay away only because she had insisted on it Sunday afternoon. He had known better than to think he could win her over by making a pest of himself. He had also hoped that after a little time alone she might be willing to let him plead his case without shutting him down completely.

But he had been too miserable to stick with his initial resolution for longer than three days. He'd had a good impersonal reason to stop by the diner that afternoon—the stuff he'd inadvertently left behind on Sunday. But the final, impossible-to-ignore spur had come from Nathan.

Awakening from his nap just a couple of hours ago, his son had climbed into his lap and looked him squarely in the eyes. Then he had asked with a heartbreaking mix of anguish and confusion that mirrored Simon's own feelings all too well, "Where Kit, Dahee? Where my Kit?"

Simon had known at that moment that neither of them could wait any longer to see her again.

"I've been a mess, too, but I was afraid if I called you or came by the diner, you'd go all prickly on me like you did Sunday afternoon. I wasn't sure I could handle getting shot down again so soon," Simon admitted.

"But you came here today anyway," Kit pointed out.

Though she had finally stopped crying, her tone was hesitant.

"I figured, what the hell? I could always pretend I'd just stopped by for my stuff. I was also going to say that Nathan was asking for you, which, in fact, he's been doing since we left here. That way I would have escaped with at least a little of my pride intact if you stomped on my heart."

"But I wouldn't do that—" she protested, then caught herself and blushed as she looked away again.

"Correct me if I'm wrong, but I seem to remember you've done just that at least once or twice already," Simon said, though not unkindly. "You called my marriage proposal *extreme,* and you certainly didn't seem to mean it in a good way. You also sent me away with my son without taking my feelings, or Nathan's, into account. Just as I thought we were becoming a family, you blithely sent us away."

"I didn't mean to be hurtful, Simon." Kit looked up at him again apologetically. "I honestly believed that you only proposed marriage out of a sense of chivalry—that you thought it was the honorable thing to do under the circumstances. My intention was to simply let you off the hook."

"Why did you feel you had to let me off the hook?" he asked, truly puzzled now. "Surely you had to know I felt more than dutiful toward you. I tried every way I could think of to show you how much I loved you."

Kit stared at him for a long, silent moment. Then she offered him a wry smile, shaking her head as if in disbelief.

"Why are you looking at me like that?" Simon demanded gruffly.

He had ventured to put his heart on the line with her one more time. He hadn't expected her to be amused.

"I've been a bit of a dunce the past couple of weeks," Kit admitted in a rueful tone. "I didn't take into account all the ways you've *shown* me how much you care. Instead I fixated on what you said, and also what you *didn't* say. Every time we talked about Lucy, you would say how much you'd *loved* her. You only ever said that you *liked* me—until just now."

"I think I fell in love with you that first day I saw you in the diner three weeks ago. You were a reminder of my past, but I knew almost at once that I wouldn't mind having you be a part of my future, too. That's why I kissed you the way I did. It just seemed so right, and I didn't even know about Nathan then." Simon hesitated, eyeing Kit warily, then decided to go for broke as he added quietly, "Of course, you've never talked abut loving me, either, and you haven't yet today."

"Oh, Simon, I do love you—I have for as long as I can remember. But you weren't mine to love," Kit said.

Putting a tender hand on his cheek, she met his gaze unflinchingly, the look in her pale eyes too forthright to be denied.

"I'm yours now, Kit," he assured her, bending his head to steal a kiss. "I'm all yours, and I do love you."

"Me, too, Dahee? Dahee love Nafan, too?" his son interjected, reminding them both of why they'd finally found the love they'd always needed.

"Yes, little buddy, I love you, too—more than I can ever say," Simon said, ruffling Nathan's dark curls with a gentle hand.

"Kit love Nafan?"

The little boy looked up at her with an engaging grin.

"Yes, sweetie, I love you so much."

She gave the little boy a hug, her eyes glinting with tears again.

"Get Nafan some juice now, Kit? Nafan want some juice."

"Of course, I'll get you some juice now, big boy." She looked at Simon again and smiled invitingly. "Will you come upstairs with me?"

"Oh, yes, Miss Kit, I have every intention of coming upstairs with you." He kissed her chastely on the cheek, then gestured to the overnight bag, computer and camera on the staircase. "I hope you weren't getting ready to dump my stuff."

"I would have never done that," she protested.

"That's good to know."

Simon collected his belongings and followed after Kit as she started up the stairs.

"I was actually on my way out to the ranch to return your things, but you got here first. I was also going to acknowledge that I'd been a silly fool, sending you away, *and* I was going to ask for your understanding and forgiveness," she admitted, her smile turning wry once more as she glanced back at him. "I made a big mistake Sunday afternoon. I was hoping I could get it right this time, but you beat me to it."

"We both got it right this time—finally," Simon said.

"Yes, finally. Will you stay for dinner?"

"I'll stay way past dinner. In fact, if you ask me nicely, I'll stay the night and have breakfast with you, too. I packed up Nathan's diaper bag, so we're both prepared."

He grinned at her as she stood aside to let him enter the apartment, pleased with the way her eyes widened not only with surprise, but also eager anticipation.

"Simon, my love, will you stay with me tonight?" she queried, the sultry voice she used ratcheting up another notch the desire that already simmered deep inside of him.

"Tonight and every night for the rest of my life, but only if you'll have me as your lawfully wedded husband."

"That sounds like a proposal of marriage to me."

"Not too *extreme,* is it?" Simon teased, sure of himself as he hadn't been the first time he'd proposed to her.

"I can't imagine where you'd get an idea like *that,*" she teased right back with a coy look.

"So is that a yes to doing me the honor of becoming my wife?"

"That's a very definite yes," she assured him.

"Juice," Nathan crowed.

He waved his teddy bear in the air, demanding his fair share of attention, as Kit and Simon looked at him and laughed.

"I'll get the diaper bag," Simon said, depositing his overnight bag, computer and camera on the living room sofa.

"And I'll get the boy some juice."

They each hesitated a moment more, gazes locked. Then Kit smiled at Simon with such love that his heart swelled near to bursting open.

"I do love you, Kit Davenport," he said.

"And I love *you,* Simon Gilmore…for now, and always…."

Epilogue

Standing just inside the French doors opening from the living room onto the back lawn at the Double Bar S, Kit looked out at the crowd of people seated on the chairs set up in rows facing the newly erected gazebo where she and Simon were about to be married. She didn't feel nearly as nervous as she'd expected to be on her wedding day.

Perhaps it was due to Mitchell Gilmore's steady presence beside her as they waited together for the string quartet to begin "The Wedding March." He had offered to give her away, and having been made to feel like family already, staying at the ranch as she had since mid-July, Kit had gladly accepted. But just as likely, the peace and serenity she felt was due in great measure to her belief in Simon, in herself and in their love for each other.

The past eight weeks had flown by in a haze of planning and preparation. Deanna and Mitchell Gilmore had welcomed the news of her engagement to their son with joy. They had given their blessing without the slightest hesitation.

They had taken over the bulk of the wedding preparations, as well, thus allowing Kit the time she'd needed to get Earl and Sylvie Eastman situated at the Dinner Belle and also pack up her belongings. She'd cared for Nathan during the week, too, while Simon went back to work in Seattle.

They'd managed to spend every weekend together, though—sometimes in Belle and sometimes in Seattle. Kit had made several trips to the city with Nathan in tow so she and Simon could look for a house centrally located to the university campus and his office near downtown.

They had found the perfect place—already vacated by the previous owners, as luck would have it. They had spent the past week moving in, returning to Belle on Friday afternoon, just in time for the wedding rehearsal and barbecue organized by Simon's parents in their honor.

Kit could hardly believe the day she and Simon had chosen almost two months ago had finally arrived. That Saturday afternoon in August couldn't have been more perfect, either. The sky stretched to the far horizon, bright and blue, and though the sun was warm, the air was cool enough to be comfortable.

The chairs were filled with people she and Simon had known all their lives, including her own special family of friends—old George, Bonnie and her family, Sara and her family, too. Winifred Averill sat in the front row with Deanna Gilmore, a smug look on her weathered face. Isaac Woodrow and his wife, Margie, were there, too, sitting next to John Mahoney and *his* wife. Just a few moments ago, Earl and Sylvie Eastman had taken a break from their catering duties and slipped into seats in the back row, as well.

The opening measures of the traditional music Kit and Simon had chosen together drifted across the lawn at last, deep and full. Mitchell gave her hand, tucked securely in the crook of his arm, a gentle squeeze.

"Ready?" he asked with a smile that reminded Kit of his son, and his grandson, too.

"Yes, all ready."

She smiled, too, smoothed a hand down the bell skirt of her simple, strapless white satin gown, took a deep breath and began her walk down the aisle left between the rows of chairs.

On either side, people stood and smiled as they watched her progress. But Kit only had eyes for Simon and his son, waiting for her hand in hand beside the minister.

Kit allowed her gaze to linger on Nathan, her smile softening. Simon's son, soon to be her son, looked so cute in his tiny tux, standing beside Simon, holding his teddy bear, also outfitted formally for the occasion. Then she met Simon's brilliant gaze and felt his lovely smile burn its way into her soul.

Pausing a moment, Mitchell turned to kiss her on the cheek, then stepped away to join Deanna, already dabbing daintily at her eyes with a lacy handkerchief. Still holding Nathan's hand, Simon stepped forward to meet her. Without any encouragement, Nathan dropped his teddy bear and took Kit's hand, bringing her and Simon together as he had so many times already.

"Dahee…look at Kit," he said, looking up at her in awe. "She vewy bootiful, isn't she?"

"Oh, yes, Nathan, our Miss Kit is very beautiful," he

said, meeting her gaze with pride as well as admiration. "Heart and soul beautiful, and that's only one of the many reasons that I love her."

"Love you, Kit…love you, *love you,* love you," Nathan chortled to the delight of everyone in attendance.

"And I love you, too—both of you—more than you'll ever know…."

* * * * *

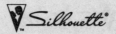

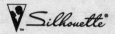

If you enjoyed what you just read,
then we've got an offer you can't resist!

Take 2 bestselling love stories FREE!
Plus get a FREE surprise gift!

Clip this page and mail it to Silhouette Reader Service™

IN U.S.A.
3010 Walden Ave.
P.O. Box 1867
Buffalo, N.Y. 14240-1867

IN CANADA
P.O. Box 609
Fort Erie, Ontario
L2A 5X3

YES! Please send me 2 free Silhouette Special Edition® novels and my free surprise gift. After receiving them, if I don't wish to receive anymore, I can return the shipping statement marked cancel. If I don't cancel, I will receive 6 brand-new novels every month, before they're available in stores! In the U.S.A., bill me at the bargain price of $4.24 plus 25¢ shipping and handling per book and applicable sales tax, if any*. In Canada, bill me at the bargain price of $4.99 plus 25¢ shipping and handling per book and applicable taxes**. That's the complete price and a savings of at least 10% off the cover prices—what a great deal! I understand that accepting the 2 free books and gift places me under no obligation ever to buy any books. I can always return a shipment and cancel at any time. Even if I never buy another book from Silhouette, the 2 free books and gift are mine to keep forever.

235 SDN DZ9D
335 SDN DZ9E

Name	(PLEASE PRINT)	
Address	Apt.#	
City	State/Prov.	Zip/Postal Code

Not valid to current Silhouette Special Edition® subscribers.

Want to try two free books from another series?
Call 1-800-873-8635 or visit www.morefreebooks.com.

 * Terms and prices subject to change without notice. Sales tax applicable in N.Y.
** Canadian residents will be charged applicable provincial taxes and GST.
   All orders subject to approval. Offer limited to one per household.
 ® are registered trademarks owned and used by the trademark owner and or its licensee.

SPED04R   ©2004 Harlequin Enterprises Limited

SPECIAL EDITION™

presents
a heartwarming NEW series!

THE HATHAWAYS
OF MORGAN CREEK:
A DYNASTY
IN THE BAKING...

NANNY IN HIDING

(SSE #1642, available October 2004)

by

Patricia Kay

On the run from her evil ex-husband, Amy Jordan
accepted blue-eyed Bryce Hathaway's offer to be his
children's nanny. This wealthy single dad was
immediately intrigued by the beautiful runaway, but if
he discovered that this caring, gentle woman was
actually a nanny *in hiding*, would he
help her out—or turn her in?

Available at your favorite retail outlet.

Receive a FREE hardcover book from

H A R L E Q U I N   R O M A N C E®

in September!

**Harlequin Romance celebrates the launch of
the line's new cover design by offering you
this exclusive offer valid only in September,
only in Harlequin Romance.**

To receive your
FREE HARDCOVER BOOK
written by bestselling author
Emilie Richards, send us four
proofs of purchase from any
September 2004 Harlequin
Romance books. Further details
and proofs of purchase can be
found in all September 2004
Harlequin Romance books.

*Must be postmarked
no later than October 31.*

**Don't forget to be one of the first
to pick up a copy of the new-look
Harlequin Romance novels in September!**

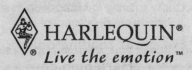

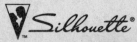
Silhouette®

COMING NEXT MONTH

SSECNM0904